MW01047550

PROPERTY OF
FRANKFORT HIGH SCHOOL

ALSO BY PAT DERBY

Visiting Miss Pierce
Goodbye Emily, Hello

PROPERTY OF
FRANKFORT HIGH SCHOOL

GRAMS,
HER BOYFRIEND,
MY FAMILY,
AND ME

PROPERTY OF
FRANKFORT HIGH SCHOOL

GRAMS, HER BOYFRIEND, MY FAMILY, AND ME

PAT DERBY

A Sunburst Book   Farrar · Straus · Giroux

PROPERTY OF
FRANKFORT HIGH SCHOOL

Copyright © 1994 by Pat Derby
All rights reserved
Published in Canada by HarperCollins*CanadaLtd*
Printed in the United States of America
First edition, 1994
Sunburst edition, 1997
Library of Congress catalog card number: 93-73169

03789

To Paul
in loving memory
and to George, Brian, and Owen
with love

GRAMS,
HER BOYFRIEND,
MY FAMILY,
AND ME

I HAVE A THEORY ABOUT FAMILIES. THE LESS YOU get involved, the less trouble you can get into. I realize you can't get along without your family, but that doesn't mean you have to get bogged down in all those stupid things families argue about. My sisters seem to love that kind of stuff. Maybe that's one of the differences between boys and girls: girls are concerned with a whole bunch of silly details. Once Ma was planning to have the bathroom painted. She and my sisters dragged home all these color cards and pieces of wallpaper and wrangled about which shade of white was the best. As far as I'm concerned, white is white and what difference does it make what's on the wall as long as the water runs and the toilet flushes.

Maybe I'm more aware of these problems because I'm surrounded by sisters. There's Dennie, who's seventeen and a senior at Bishop Alemany High School. She's always telling me I'm insensitive. My sister Molly is such a pint-sized genius that at thirteen she's already a freshman at Bishop Alemany. I'm a sophomore, and I hope they don't let kids skip grades in high school, because I couldn't take it if Molly and I were in the same class. Then there are the twins, Alice and Anne, who are six years old and in the first grade at St. Edward's Grammar School.

Before the twins came, I had my own room, one of the perks of being the only boy in my family. But when the twins were born, Ma and Pop actually put them in with me.

"Don't worry, Andy," Ma said. "They're tiny babies and their cribs won't take up much space. Besides, it's only temporary."

Now, we're not talking about a huge room here. It was already full of my stuff. That's when I should have padlocked my door, because before I knew it, their little cribs had turned into big cribs, and then their toys started to appear. Ma suggested it would be much better if I moved my smelly model glue and dangerous baseball bat out. She actually said, "I think they belong in the garage before someone gets hurt." Next she said she was afraid the twins would break my fragile CD player, and it was moved to the living room. My clothes ended up in the hall linen closet. I began to feel like one of those homeless people on the streets, drifting from place to place with nowhere to settle permanently.

Ma and Pop kept saying they would have to do something about it, but all I ever heard was "Next year."

Finally Dennie said, "Ma, it's practically indecent! Andy can't share his room with the twins anymore. What will my friends say?"

"Yeah," I agreed.

That's how I ended up in the room off the kitchen. I guess

it could be called a sort of porch—we'd used it mostly as a storage area and back entry to the garage. There are three drawbacks. Daisy, our dog, considers it her doghouse, since she had possession of it before I did; people still use it as a passageway; and it's impossible to sleep in late because I can hear everything that goes on in the kitchen. The pluses are I have my own space again, my CD player is back, and both doors lock, so I can just shut the family out.

My policy of noninvolvement worked pretty well. Mostly I either agreed with things that didn't affect me, like the color of the bathroom, or I ignored whatever the family was arguing about. But my strategy stopped working when Ma decided to get a job.

It all started the second week of September. I was lying in bed, half-asleep, with Daisy breathing her smelly doggy breath in my face. My digital clock flashed 6:07. School had been in session for two weeks, and I figured, since I had thirty-six minutes before I had to get up, it was worth going back to sleep. I had pulled the covers over my face when Daisy started to growl softly, whipping her tail around and dragging the blankets off my feet.

"Knock it off," I said. Then I heard Ma and Dennie talking.

"If we jog eight blocks over to Nineteenth Avenue and back, I think that will be enough for my first time," Ma was saying.

"No sweat, Mom, you can do it," Dennie said. "It's not much harder than taking a walk."

"That's fine for you," Ma said. "But I usually don't even walk that far."

"Walk" seemed to be the operative word because Daisy leaped off my bed and flung herself against the door.

I leaned over and opened it. That gives you a good idea of how big my room is. Daisy galloped out.

"Did we wake you, Andy?" Ma called.

"It's okay," I said.

"Come on, Daisy, want to go with us?" I heard Dennie snap her fingers to get Daisy's attention.

Daisy yelped in agreement.

I rolled over, but it was too late—I was completely awake. I decided to grab the bathroom before anyone else got it. Did I mention we only have one bathroom?

Pop must have had the same idea because I met him in the hallway.

"Not out jogging?" I asked.

"Not on your life. I'll leave that to the distaff side," Pop said. "You use the bathroom; I'll make coffee for your mother."

By the time Ma and Dennie came back, the coffee was ready, the twins and Molly were fighting for space in the bathroom, and Pop and I were eating breakfast.

"You've got to come jogging with us tomorrow, Chris," Ma said to Pop. "It's a marvelous way to start the day—it really clears out your head."

"I'll stick to coffee. Thanks, anyway," Pop said. He took a sip. "What's up for today?"

Molly came into the kitchen with her toothbrush in her hand. "Mom," she said. "Make the twins get out of the bathroom."

Ma ignored Molly's request. "I'm glad you asked that question," she said to Pop. "I wasn't going to bring it up right now, but since most of us are here, I want to tell you what I've been thinking about. Since the twins are in school, and both Dennie and Andy will be in college soon, we can certainly use more money. Anyway, I'd like to get a job."

"Mom! That's great!" Dennie said. "Good for you. It's time you did something for yourself."

"It would take some adjustments," Ma said. "What do you think of the idea, Chris?"

"A job! What kind of a job?" Pop didn't look at Ma. He just stirred his coffee.

"My friend Nina works at a real estate office. Their receptionist is quitting. She's sure she can get me the job. It doesn't pay a lot to start, but if I like the field, I might be able to move into selling. Of course, then I'd have to take classes in real estate. But to start, being a receptionist would be fine."

I was amazed that Ma would just spring this idea on Pop. He doesn't like surprises. He says he wants to know where he is at all times. Ma says he's not very flexible.

"It's worth a try, I guess," Pop said.

"Good!" Ma glanced around the table. "You're all going to have to help, you understand."

Dennie looked at her watch. "Yikes, I better take my shower. I'll be glad to help, but don't forget, I'm editor of the school paper and I have my job at F.C. for G.P.L."

That was how Dennie referred to the shop where she worked. Actually it was called Friendly Clothes for Generously Proportioned Ladies. I'm not sure why the managers hired Dennie—she certainly is not generously proportioned. In fact, a lot of the time she looks downright skinny to me.

"What kind of help are you talking about?" Molly asked suspiciously.

"Oh, not a lot," Ma said. "Turning on the oven and the washer and dryer. Maybe folding the clothes, dusting, picking up the twins after school."

"That's what I thought," Molly said. "Well, I'm not going

to be the only one who does it. Andy and Dennie have to do some stuff, too. Fair's fair."

I didn't say anything. I planned to be busy with soccer practice. I turned to Molly. "Are you coming with me, or are you going to get a ride to school with Dennie and Bruce?" Bruce is Dennie's latest boyfriend.

"I'd rather go with you," Molly said.

Bruce usually drives Dennie to school in his old Volkswagen. He's lasted longer than any of her other boyfriends. I don't think he's too bright, but at least he doesn't pat me on the head and call me a worm, the way one of her other boyfriends did.

"Is Bruce still around?" Pop asked.

Pop can't stand Bruce. I'm not sure why, but then Pop can be funny about people. He'll take a dislike to someone and there's no changing his mind. He never seems to like any of Dennie's boyfriends. He frowns at them and grumbles and asks them a lot of embarrassing questions. Eventually they stop coming over. Dennie will be really mad for a while, but then she'll find some other guy.

Molly ignored Pop's question. "Honestly, Mom, why can't I go to school by myself? I feel as if Andy is my duenna. This is the 1990s, you know."

I didn't know what a duenna was, but I wouldn't give Molly the satisfaction of letting her know that. A few weeks of Spanish and Molly thinks she knows everything. I looked it up later. I couldn't be a duenna; it's from the Spanish for an elderly chaperone for young girls.

Ma sighed. "Molly, we've gone over this since school started. You're a year younger than the rest of your class, and it's a very rough neighborhood the public bus goes through, and little girls, especially little girls wearing uniforms, seem to be the target for troublemakers."

What I don't understand is why it isn't safe in the morning but Molly is allowed to come home by herself after school. Ma's tried to explain that it is light in the afternoon and that there are more people about. It doesn't make much sense to me, but Ma has a lot of strange ideas like that. Whenever we change to daylight saving time, she keeps talking about "real" time and "fake" time.

"I'm leaving in five minutes," I said to Molly. "You'd better be ready."

Molly picked up her toothbrush and stomped out of the kitchen. I could hear her pounding on the bathroom door and yelling at Dennie to give somebody else a chance at the bathroom.

I gathered my books off the table, loaded my backpack, and went to the front door and opened it. I looked down the street. "Clean teeth or not," I yelled, "the bus is a block away. Get a move on or I'm leaving."

Molly came running down the hallway, balancing her coat and books on her arm. Luckily, she's too young to be allowed to wear all that junk girls put on their faces, so it doesn't take her long to get ready. She's not like Dennie, who won't leave her room, much less the house, unless everything is absolutely perfect. Once Dennie refused to go to a family dinner because she had just gotten her hair cut and the hairdresser cut it too short. She sulked around the house for over a week with her head tied up in a bandanna.

"Well, come on." Molly went through the front door and down the stairs. She started running.

I hate to admit it, but Molly can run faster than I can. She raced the bus to the corner and then held it for me by standing in the doorway. She was just showing off.

I passed her and got on the bus. Molly and I never sit together. If the bus is crowded, I tell Molly to stand near the front. Then I move to the middle and watch her from there. If the bus isn't crowded, I sit where I can see her. When we get off at school, I always walk behind her so people won't think we're together.

Today, though, she waited for me.

"What do you want?" I said.

"Don't worry, I won't tell your stupid friends you're my bodyguard. I just wanted to ask you what you thought of Mom going back to work."

I shrugged. "It's not going to affect me. If it makes her happy, why not?"

"Hah. Someday you'll need clean clothes and they won't be there," she said. Then she went to join some of her friends. Why are girls always trying to complicate things?

AT LUNCHTIME, I FOUND MOLLY AT MY LOCKER.
The freshman lockers are up on the second floor, so it was
unusual to see her hanging around mine.

"Now what do you want?" I asked.

"Would you mind if I talked to your friend Martin?"

"Why do you want to talk to Martin?" I asked. "What's he
got to do with you?"

"His sister Jennie said he took the Bay Area social concerns
class last year."

Bishop Alemany is a Catholic high school in San Francisco.
It has weird religion classes like the one Molly was talking
about. I didn't take it last year when I was a freshman, because
my reading skills were so abysmal, according to my counselor,
that I had to take remedial reading instead. Another weird class
is the one Dennie's taking: death and dying. My religion class
this semester is modern social issues.

"Don't tell me you're taking that stupid class," I said.

"Nobody told me not to," Molly said. "How was I supposed to know I'd have to do some crummy community project? You should have warned me."

"I never took that class," I said. But I remembered that the teacher, a replacement for an old nun who has since retired, made everybody find some community project to do. Martin went to a place called Cherry Garden Convalescent Hospital to visit an elderly man. Martin complained about that class for the whole semester. I slammed my locker door closed. "What do you expect to find out from Martin?"

"Ms. Jackson said that the convalescent hospital was available to us again, and I just wondered if I should go there or try to think of some other project for the class."

"I'll talk to him," I said. I hoped Molly wasn't going to start thinking that because we were in the same high school, my friends were going to be her friends. Dennie won't let me talk to her friends, either.

"You won't forget, will you? I need to choose a project by tomorrow."

"Don't worry," I said.

I mentioned to Martin that Molly was worried about the class, and he laughed. "Tell her not to worry. Ms. Jackson is back this year and she's a pushover. Last year, whoever turned in a report got at least a B."

When I got home that afternoon, Ma was sitting at the kitchen table drinking a cup of coffee. I dropped my gym bag on the floor. "Hi," I said.

She looked up. "Hi, yourself." She wrinkled her nose. "Andy, what is in that bag? I can smell it from here."

"Just the usual," I said. "Towels, socks, underwear, gym shorts, knee pads."

"And I guess you expect it all washed and dried by tomorrow morning?"

"Well," I said. "The coach told us to clean out our gym lockers and bring our stuff back tomorrow."

"And who did your coach think was going to wash this stuff?"

I looked at her. "I guess I could wash them myself." I leaned over to pick up my bag. I kept expecting her to smile and say, "Only kidding." Instead she said, "Good idea! Consider it a learning experience. By the way, the washer and dryer are in the garage."

"I know that." Carrying the gym bag, I went through my room and out the back door, down the stairs, and into the garage. A lot of houses in San Francisco look like ours. All the houses on the block are stuck together with no space between them. The garages are on the street level and the houses are built over them. They aren't big places.

Now, I'm not one of those dopey males who can't use appliances. Last year B.A. offered as an elective this incredibly stupid class called bachelor living. The idea was that boys should be capable of surviving on their own. I took it because I thought it would be an easy A. It was. Our final was baking a cake.

Anyway, along with being able to construct a lopsided chocolate cake, I learned how to use a washing machine. But my theory is, why do something if you can get somebody else to do it?

Today, though, looked like one of those times I would have to use my expertise. I threw my gym bag down and lifted the lid of the washer. It was full of clean, wet clothes. I opened the door of the dryer. It was full of clean, dry clothes. If our coach hadn't told us he would give a demerit to anyone who wasn't completely suited out, I would have left the bag and hoped for the best. I was sure Ma wouldn't let it sit there forever.

I started to drag the clothes out of the dryer and dump them in a basket as Molly, pulling Daisy by her leash, came through the side door of the garage.

"I don't believe it!" she exclaimed. "Do my eyes deceive me? No, it can't be, my macho brother doing the wash?"

"Funny," I said and pushed Daisy away with my foot.

"This is just the beginning, you realize." Molly picked up one of her socks from the basket and started pawing through the pile for the other one.

"What are you talking about?" I asked.

"Wait until Mom's really at work, that's what I'm talking about. Almost everybody I know has a mother who works, and my friends are always having to cook or clean or baby-sit."

"Don't sweat it." I shoveled the wet clothes into the dryer, slammed the door, set the timer, and pushed the start button.

"I hope you add some bleach to that smelly stuff," Molly said, watching me dump the contents of my gym bag into the washer. "Did you get a chance to talk to Martin?"

"Yeah, he said don't worry. Ms. Jackson gives B's for just doing the minimum."

"That's not what I asked you to do," Molly said. "I always get good grades. I want to know if I should go to that convalescent hospital."

I realized I had forgotten to ask that. "Why not?" I said. "It saves you trying to invent some other project."

"I guess." Molly tugged on Daisy's leash and started up the stairs.

"My room is not a hallway," I called, but Daisy and Molly had already disappeared.

At dinner that night, Ma said, "I told my friend Nina at the real estate office I was definitely interested in the job. I'm supposed to go in tomorrow for an interview with the manager."

"What are you going to wear?" Dennie asked.

"What do you think of my brown dress and white jacket?"

Dennie nodded. "It's okay," she said. "Not great, but passable. You're going to need more clothes."

"If I get this job, I'm not going to start spending money on new clothes," Ma said. "That's not the point of my going back to work."

"Come on, Mom, loosen up. You need clothes that are businesslike and sophisticated. You've still got a pretty good figure, considering."

"Your mother looks fine," Pop said.

Dennie ignored him. "I don't work this Friday night. I'll take you shopping. You have to start thinking about yourself, stop being a slave to us."

"Speak for yourself," Molly said. "You'll be gone soon. Mom wasn't working when you were a freshman in high school."

"The twins were just babies then," Dennie said. "Mom might as well have been working. Who do you think did all the washing?"

"They wore disposable diapers," Molly said.

"Girls, girls." Pop raised his voice to be heard over Molly and Dennie's arguing. "Stop it. After all, it's important that a family stick together. Now, we all want your mother to be happy, don't we?"

"I'm not unhappy," Ma said. "But thank you for your concern."

"You don't have to thank Dad," Dennie said. "You're not a

child who needs permission to do something. Women have the same rights as men."

"I didn't say anything like that," Pop interrupted.

"Geez, Dennie," Molly said. "You sound like you're making a speech. When you and Bruce go out, do you insist on paying for everything?"

"A lot you know," Dennie said.

At that point, Alice spilled her milk.

"That's it," Pop yelled, jumping up as the milk started dripping onto his lap. "Can't we have one meal without some-body spilling their milk?"

It was a question that I had heard for years. Nobody even considered answering it.

"I'll take care of it," Ma said.

By the time the table and Alice had been mopped up, and Pop had wiped off his pants, the subject had been changed. Pop was questioning us to find out who had left the side door unlocked again. "Anybody could just walk in off the street and steal us blind," he said.

Pop's always worrying about people breaking in. I think if he could get away with it, he would build a moat around our house and have a drawbridge.

"Not to mention killing us in our beds," Ma chimed in.

On that pleasant note we finished dinner. As I started to get up, Ma said, "I'd like to talk to all of you for a few minutes. We need to discuss something."

"Should we stay, too?" the twins asked in unison.

"Yes, this concerns everybody," Ma replied. "Before I com-mit myself to this job, I want to be sure it's feasible. The main thing I have to know is that Anne and Alice are taken care of after school."

"But we can't do that," Dennie said. "The twins are out of

school at two-thirty and we aren't out until three. Even if we left school the minute the bell rings, it's a good thirty minutes before we can get home. And some days I have meetings for the newspaper staff."

"All the clubs meet after school," Molly added.

"What clubs do you belong to?" I asked.

"None yet. But I plan to join some as soon as I find the ones I like."

"Well, I have soccer," I said. Soccer is a winter sport at Bishop Alemany, but if you want to get on the team, you'd better show up for all the practices, even the unofficial ones the coach calls. He claims he wants to be sure his players are truly committed.

"Just stop for a minute," Ma said. "I haven't finished. I know when Bishop Alemany gets out. I've talked to Mrs. Kennedy, Susie's mother, and she has agreed to take the twins home with her after school. The girls can play with Susie. But I am not going to impose on her. I promised her that the twins would be picked up by four. That will give one of you plenty of time to get them. You can't all be staying after school every day. So, as I was saying, there are certain jobs around the house that have to be done. But the main thing is the twins. At first I was going to make up a schedule, but then your father and I talked and we decided to allow you to make your own arrange-ments."

"That's not fair," Molly said. She always says that. "I don't know when I'll have to stay at school. Dennie knows when the paper meets, and Andy must know when practices are."

"What do we have to do?" Anne asked.

"Mind your business," I said.

"Be nice and polite when you're at Susie's and be sure to keep your room clean," Ma said. "And the rest of you, don't start arguing and fighting about things now. If we discover something isn't working, we can discuss it again."

Discuss what again? It didn't seem to me we had discussed anything at all. I got up and went downstairs to put my gym clothes into the dryer. First things first.

3

IT'S FUNNY HOW WHAT GOES ON IN REAL LIFE sometimes comes up in class. Which is what happened the next day in my modern social issues class. It's a pretty boring class. Already we've had to read a couple of essays written a thousand years ago. There are words in those essays I can't even pronounce. The sentences are so long and complicated that when I read them, I feel as if I'm translating a foreign language.

Mr. Archer, the teacher, is always asking questions like, "What's more important, the good of the individual or the good of society?" Come on. I'm barely fifteen years old. How should I know?

Today Freddy Miles brought up an interesting point. Mr. Archer had just been explaining that society is divided into smaller units like countries, states, cities, and families. "Take your own family," Mr. Archer said. "Do you think it functions as a unit?"

Freddy raised his hand. "Hey, like you mean everybody is supposed to think of the family and not themselves?"

"Excellent!" Mr. Archer exclaimed. Mr. Archer gets excited about anything. "The family should be a perfect example of people working together. The father works—"

"Mr. Archer, Mr. Archer!" Rita Silveria yelled from the back of the room. "What about women? Don't they work?"

"Traditionally, while women certainly worked at home, since there was no pay involved . . ." Mr. Archer started to say, but he was drowned out by a bunch of the girls protesting.

"Mr. Archer?" Freddy shouted. "Take vacations. Say the father wants to go on a fishing trip and the mother wants to go to Hawaii and I want to go to Tahoe and my dumb sister wants to go to a computer camp and my little brother wants to go to Disneyland, how can everybody work as a unit? What's fair about that?"

"What do you bet old Mom doesn't get to go to Hawaii," Rita said. "Let's dump on Mom."

"No," Lucy Carey said. "I can see what Mr. Archer is talking about. If people did only what they wanted, nothing would work. I mean, who wants to cook and clean?"

"Yeah," Freddy chimed in. "And work like a dog every day and not be able to spend the money on yourself because you have to give it to your wife so she can go shopping for clothes."

Rita stood up and leaned across her neighbor's desk. "Listen, creep," she said. "Women cook and clean and then work like dogs outside the house."

"Rita, sit down," Mr. Archer yelled. "You people are a good example of what life would be like if everybody was only interested in himself." He glanced at the clock. "For homework, I want each of you to write an essay predicting what life—"

The bell interrupted him. "Just wait a minute." He held up his hand. ". . . will be like in fifty years if people continue to be self-centered."

Most of the kids had gathered their books and were headed toward the door.

"Written double-spaced in ink," he shouted after us.

"Mr. Archer lives in the dark ages. 'Women traditionally stay home,'" Rita said, mimicking the teacher's voice. "Honestly!"

I nodded at Rita. She's not the sort of person I wanted to argue with.

Ma got the job and almost immediately things started to fall apart. "I don't care how you arrange your schedules, but somebody better be free at four," she said. Then she added that it was time we grew up and became responsible.

It wasn't easy to get Dennie and Molly to be reasonable. Dennie acted as if being a senior was all the excuse she needed for not doing her fair share. Molly kept repeating, "I'm not doing everything," whenever I pointed out that she was the only one with a flexible calendar. Both Molly and Dennie said they couldn't understand why I was being so paranoid about soccer practice when the coach wasn't going to pick the team until after Christmas. They refused to understand that unless I demonstrated a certain willingness to be always available, I wouldn't make the first cut. Dennie said that if I was any good, the coach would be glad to have me under any circumstances.

The first week was total chaos. Monday was Dennie's turn, but at noon there was some emergency with the printer for the school paper. She couldn't find me, so she got Molly to collect the twins. We had agreed Molly's day would be Tuesday for that week. Wednesday and Friday were supposed to be my turn. I did Wednesday all right, but on Thursday Martin and I were fooling around in the cafeteria during lunchtime and we spilled a little food. Big deal. But we both ended up with Friday afternoon detention. I figured Dennie hadn't done Monday, so on Thursday night I told her it was her turn to collect them. Dennie said she had traded with Molly and what they did was none of my business. Molly said she wouldn't do it; she had already done her share. Finally Pop said he couldn't stand to listen to all this fighting and, for the sake of a little peace, he supposed he could leave work early on Friday. But he would do it just this once. We kids would have to get organized and start pulling together. He made us sound like a team of horses.

It was a real pain having everything so mixed up. And it didn't get any better. One morning after Ma had been working about six weeks, Dennie banged on my door. "Let me in," she yelled. "I want to go to the garage. I think my running shoes are in the dryer." She rattled the knob. "Honestly, you shouldn't lock yourself in. Suppose there was a fire?"

"Go away," I snarled. "My room is not a hallway."

"I'm not going outside in my bare feet."

I sighed and unlocked my door. Daisy bolted out and Dennie came in. "I'll go out the garage," she called to Ma. "Meet you in front."

I buried my head under my pillow. "It wouldn't hurt you to jog, too," Dennie said. "Maybe you could develop some muscles."

I grunted. After Dennie left, it was quiet for a few minutes and then I heard Pop in the kitchen. I gave up trying to get back to sleep and got up.

"Sorry, son," Pop said when he saw me. "Did I wake you?"

"Nah, Dennie did that." I wandered over to the refrigerator, opened the door, and pulled out a carton of milk. "What are you doing up so early?"

Pop had a bunch of vegetables on the counter. "I told your mother I'd get the stew ready for the slow cooker."

I was surprised. This wasn't like Pop at all. I guess he decided it would be easier to get the meal ready himself than to eat at nine o'clock because one of us forgot to defrost the dinner. The quality of our meals had gone way down. Now, frankly, I don't care. As long as there's enough of it and the catsup bottle is handy, I can make do. But Pop considers himself something of a gourmet. He likes Ma to experiment, even when some of her experiments don't always work out.

I pulled a box of cereal off a shelf. There were no cereal bowls in the cabinet, so I opened the dishwasher, inspected a bowl, decided it had been washed, and put it on the table.

Pop looked at me and raised one eyebrow. "You know, kid, you could hustle a bit more. Why don't you empty the dishwasher and put the dishes away?"

"I will." I poured some flakes into my bowl.

"You are a member of this family." Pop stopped chopping to examine one of his fingers. "Damn!" He went over to the sink and turned on the water.

"We were talking about that in school a while ago," I said. "How the family is a basic unit or something."

Pop nodded. "Everybody doing their fair share. I'll be honest, son: do you really think you're doing yours?" He dried his finger and went to the cupboard to get a Band-Aid.

I wondered what Pop would say if I suggested that maybe our unit would work better if Ma stayed home. But it was early in the morning, and I really didn't want to get into such a heavy conversation. It wouldn't hurt, though, to test the subject.

"Do we really need more money?" I asked.

"That's not the point," Pop said.

"Right." I dumped my dish in the sink. I figured I'd better hit the bathroom before Dennie and Ma got back. Since Ma had started working, she was as bad as Dennie, tying up the bathroom while she did stuff to herself. Sometimes when I would catch a quick glimpse of her, I wouldn't even recognize her. Her hair looked different and she had junk on her face and she had on high-heeled shoes.

"And where are you going?" Pop asked.

"To the bathroom?"

"Not until you put those dishes away and rinse that bowl."

As I turned back, I heard the bathroom door slam. Molly was up and I had lost my turn.

4

WITH ALL THE TRADING WE WERE DOING, OUR schedules became so complicated that nobody was sure who was supposed to be doing what. Which is how, I guess, the twins got lost. Well, not lost exactly, more like misplaced.

I think it was Dennie's turn. I know it wasn't mine because I had had them the day before. I remember that very clearly, since it had been a bad day for me. The coach had called another extra pickup practice for after school. I didn't even try to negotiate with Molly and Dennie. I didn't want to end up owing either one of them. I thought it would be simpler to make my own arrangements.

So I talked David, a junior on the team, into driving me over to Mrs. Kennedy's, where I picked up the twins and brought them back to school. I told them they were to sit on the bleachers and not to move so much as a muscle or, not only would I kill them, I would steal their favorite stuffed animals

25

and flush them one by one down the toilet! That got their attention, and for a while they sat on the bleachers and watched the practice.

None of the guys, except David, knew I was baby-sitting. Then some of the girls who were hanging around the field started playing with them.

"Wow, look!" one of the girls said. "Twins. Aren't they adorable."

That's all Alice and Anne needed. They started acting silly and super-cute so the girls would give them more compliments, and before I knew it, they were running up and down the bleachers. Then Alice fell and started screaming.

"That does it!" the coach yelled. "Who owns those kids?"

"I do," I said. I figured I might as well be honest. Besides, there was no way I could deny they were my sisters.

"I'm sure this will come as a big surprise to you, Mr. Halliday, but this is a soccer practice, not a daycare center. I'll give you five minutes to get those kids out of here."

I looked around and recognized a girl who had homeroom with me last year. She was the only one whose name I knew.

"Hey, Karen," I called. "Do me a favor and keep an eye on these two for fifteen or twenty minutes?"

"Why?" Karen asked.

"Why?" Her reply surprised me. "Because I'd appreciate it?"

The expression on her face didn't change.

I tried again. "Because you want to support the sports program?"

She frowned and then shook her head.

"I'll pay you. How much do you want?"

"I get five dollars an hour for baby-sitting. Give me a dollar fifty."

"You have a deal." I grabbed a twin with each hand. "Take them and keep them from doing any expensive damage."

By the time practice was over, the twins were collected, and I'd gotten home, I was pretty annoyed. The twins were really complicating my life. So, the next morning, when I heard Dennie trying to find somebody to trade with, I beat a quick retreat.

"I can't," I heard Molly saying. "Ask Andy."

Don't ask Andy, I muttered under my breath and quietly shut the front door.

Dennie opened the door and shouted after me, "Andy! Wait a minute."

"I can't do it!" I yelled back at her.

"Yes you can, you have to." She slammed the door.

"No way," I said to myself. I didn't even wait for Molly.

It was almost six when I got home. I dumped my books on my bed and went into the kitchen to get some milk.

"Andy, is that you?" Dennie was standing at the sink.

"So?"

"Where are the twins?" she asked.

"How should I know. It was your turn, or maybe it was Molly's turn. It wasn't my turn." I opened the refrigerator. It suddenly occurred to me that Dennie had been crying. "What's the matter?"

"We don't know where the twins are," she said.

"What do you mean?"

"It's very complicated," Dennie said. "Mrs. Kennedy phoned Mom yesterday to say she couldn't mind them today, she had to take Susie to the dentist, and one of us would have to pick them up at school. I told you that this morning."

27

"You never told me anything this morning. Besides, how could one of us pick them up after school? We don't get out at the same time they do."

"Mom made arrangements to let them stay with the older kids in that after-school tutoring program. It was just for today. When I got home about a half hour ago and realized you were still at school, Bruce and I drove over to St. Edward's. The teacher told me she never saw them, so she figured we had made other arrangements. Maybe they decided to walk home. Bruce is driving around the neighborhood now."

"How come if it wasn't your turn you're so worried about them?" I asked. "Where's Molly? Maybe she has them."

"She stayed at school for a Science Club meeting. She got home a few minutes ago. She's looking in the park."

"Do they know the way home?" I said.

"I don't know. Andy, what are we going to do? Should we call the police?"

"Maybe we should call some of their friends first?" I suggested.

"Do you know any of their friends' names?"

"Of course not." Actually, until then, I didn't think of the twins having any friends, except for Susie, of course.

"Maybe Susie knows where they went," I said. "Is she back from the dentist yet?"

"I was too embarrassed to phone," Dennie said. "You phone."

I gave her a disgusted look.

Most people have phones in the kitchen. A lot of people have phones all over the house. But when my folks bought the house, the phone was in the hall, and there it's stayed. It's not exactly convenient. It means if you're in the kitchen, you have to go through the dining room and living room to get to it.

Ma had stuck a note with the Kennedys' phone number on the bulletin board above the phone table. I dialed the number.

"Mrs. Kennedy?" I asked. "This is Andy Halliday, yeah, fine. Listen, we seem to have our messages mixed up. Did you see the twins after school?" I paused to let her talk. "Yes, I know you were taking Susie to the dentist. It's just that they weren't at the after-school program and I wondered if you or Susie had seen them."

"What is she saying?" Dennie asked, hovering at my side.

"Be quiet," I whispered. "She's talking to Susie." There was another pause, and then Susie came on the line. "Hi, Susie," I said. "Listen, did Anne and Alice say where they were going? Billy Smythe. Okay, great. Put your mother back on the phone."

"What is it?" Dennie tugged at my shirt.

"Shut up," I said. "Oh, hi, Mrs. Kennedy, no, not you. Do you have any idea what Billy Smythe's phone number or address is? Sure, I'll wait." I turned to Dennie. "Susie said she saw them talking to Billy Smythe. Mrs. Kennedy is looking up his phone number for me. Hand me a pencil."

Dennie started to say something, but I raised my hand to stop her. "555-6754. Right, no, no. I'm sure everything is all right. Yes, we'll let you know if anything is wrong. Oh," I added, "thanks."

I hung up. "I guess we should phone Billy."

"What if Billy never saw them or doesn't know where they went?" Dennie started pacing up and down the hall. "Why didn't you get them like I asked?"

"I told you I couldn't." I picked up the receiver and dialed Billy's number.

"The line's busy." I hung up and then stared at the phone. "Maybe we should call the police after all."

Now Dennie was the one who hesitated. "That seems so drastic," she said.

In the middle of this discussion, Molly arrived. "I couldn't find them and nobody in the park says they saw twins," she said. "And Mom's coming."

"What'll we tell her?" Dennie asked.

"We could say we went to get them and they weren't there," Molly said. "We don't have to tell her we were a little late."

"Like a couple of hours," I said.

We heard the garage door open. Molly and Dennie started to cry. Even I had a funny feeling in the pit of my stomach as if an ice cube had been dropped down my throat.

"If anything has happened to them, I'll never forgive myself," Dennie said. "Or you either." She looked at me.

We heard Ma's footsteps on the back stairs and the outside door of my room open. "And what," she asked, "do you three have to say for yourselves?"

WHEN MOLLY SAW MA, SHE STARTED WAILING AND then she threw her arms around Ma. "We're sorry, we're sorry."

Ma peeled Molly's arms from around her neck. "I'm sure," she said.

"We didn't mean to be late picking up the twins," Dennie said. "I thought Andy was doing it."

"That's a lie," I yelled. "I never said I would do it."

"Just listen to yourselves," Ma interrupted. "I can't believe you. For all you know, the twins might have been hurt or kidnapped, and here you three stand, arguing and fighting about whose turn it was to watch them."

Dennie sniffed. "We were doing something. We were going to call the police and Andy phoned Mrs. Kennedy and Susie saw them talking to Billy Smythe and Bruce is out driving around looking for them."

31

"Wait a minute," I said. I suddenly realized that Ma didn't seem to be very upset. "You know the twins are all right, don't you?"

Ma ignored me. "You are very, very lucky," she said. "Billy invited them home to play, and when his mother recognized them, she phoned me at work. She had a feeling they weren't where they were supposed to be."

"They just went off with Billy after everything you said about never, never going anywhere with anyone but family?" Molly asked.

"Oh, please," Ma said. "Don't try to put the blame for this on the twins." She turned to Dennie. "When Bruce reports in, will you two go over to the Smythes' and pick them up. I have the address here."

Dennie took the slip of paper and went off. I heard the bathroom door close. I guess she wanted to fix herself up before Bruce got back.

"Andy, go down and get the groceries from the car," Ma said.

I quickly disappeared. I could hear Molly's and Ma's voices as I went through my room. Words like "responsible," and "common sense," and "growing up" drifted behind me. I took my time hauling the grocery bags out of the car.

When Pop got home, he and Ma went into their bedroom. I wondered how bad Ma made the story sound, because when he came out of the bedroom, he didn't even look at the rest of us.

Dinner that night was grim. The only ones talking were the twins and Bruce. Once Bruce gets into the house, he's difficult to move out. He has a habit of hanging around until Ma finally asks him to stay to dinner. Pop doesn't approve of that. But there Bruce was sitting at the table taking the last four pieces of bacon. The rest of us played with our scrambled eggs. No one had thought to put the casserole in the oven.

The twins kept rattling on about Billy's house.

"He has white rats and three snakes," Anne said.

"One snake hung from the bookcase. It was this long." Alice held up her hands and spread them as far apart as they would go.

"Hey, kid." Bruce raised his fork. "What kind of snake was it?"

Dennie shivered. "This is a disgusting conversation for the dinner table."

"Why can't we have a snake?" Anne asked.

"We don't have any room," Dennie replied.

Molly kept sniffing and her nose and eyes were red. I guess her discussion with Ma hadn't gone very well. I wondered if Ma had decided that Molly was to blame or if Dennie and I were in for a lecture, too.

I should have been suspicious of Ma and Pop. They were too quiet. After dinner, Dennie and Molly almost fell over themselves clearing the table.

Dennie even threw Bruce the broom.

"What's this?" he asked.

"A broom," Molly answered. "You sweep with it. You know, you move all the dust and crumbs into a pile and then you pick them up in a dustpan."

"Yeah?" He just stood there.

"You eat, you sweep," Molly said.

"I tell you, Bruce," Ma finally said, "the family, including Dennie, are planning on having a conference tonight. I'll let you off the hook. You run along and Dennie will see you tomorrow."

"Mother! How can you." Dennie put down the dish towel.

"Very easily," Ma said. "Goodbye, Bruce."

"Good night," Bruce said. He glanced over at Dennie, who shrugged her shoulders.

"Now." Ma motioned Dennie and Molly to sit down. "Let's talk."

Anne and Alice started to wiggle off their chairs.

"Stay where you are," Ma said. "You weren't exactly angels today, you know."

Pop coughed slightly. "They're only four—" he started to say, but Ma interrupted.

"They're six," she said. "And they know the rules. What happened today was unforgivable. I can't tell you how disappointed I am in the lot of you."

"That's not fair," I said. "It wasn't—"

"Spare me." Ma raised her hand to stop me. "You're as bad as the others. In fact, I think we are all at fault."

"All?" Pop said.

"Well, some more than others," Ma conceded. "I realize now that part of this mess is my fault."

I gave a sigh of relief. When parents start taking some of the blame, the heat is off the kids.

"I should have realized that I wasn't . . ." She paused.

"Understanding enough?" Molly suggested.

Ma frowned. "No, that wasn't what I was going to say. I wasn't firm enough. You children need to understand how important it is for all of you to become more responsible."

Things stopped looking so good. We were already demoted to children.

Pop cleared his throat. "Your mother and I discussed this, and we decided that you three can sit at this table until you've come up with a workable plan that assures us the twins are picked up on time."

34

"I have a paper . . ." I started to say.

"Fine." Ma got up. "Then you'd better get cracking."

"Ah, Mom?" Dennie asked.

We never found out what Dennie was going to say because the phone rang. Pop got up to answer it.

"Mother?" we heard him say loudly. "Your voice sounds funny. What's the matter?"

We stopped talking and started trying to listen.

"You what?" Pop asked. "Are you all right? Mother, stop crying. I can't understand you when you cry. No, no, don't be foolish."

By this time the six of us had crowded into the hall.

"Chris, what happened?" Ma whispered.

Pop held the receiver away from his ear. He covered the mouthpiece with his hand. "There was a small fire at her house. She seems to have hurt her wrist. She's at the hospital."

"Good heavens," Ma said.

Grams is Pop's mother. She lives in this old Victorian-style house in Alameda, a city across the Bay from San Francisco. Grams is always saying to us, "Why do you people keep living in that tiny little house? I have plenty of room. Come live with me."

Once I heard Ma say to Pop, "Over my dead body." I'm glad that's the way she feels. If we moved to Alameda, I'd have to change schools and Pop would have to commute. He hates the time he spends getting to work as it is. I can't imagine what mood he'd be in if it took him twice as long and if he had to go over the Bay Bridge besides.

"I'm leaving right now," Pop said into the receiver. "I realize you can't go home because it's full of water, but we're certainly not going to abandon you. I'll be there in less than an hour. Yes, I'll stop by the house and pick up some of your clothes."

Pop pantomimed his need for pencil and paper. Ma rummaged in the phone table drawer and handed them to him.

After scribbling for a few minutes, Pop hung up the phone and went back into the kitchen. We trailed behind him.

"What happened?" Dennie said.

"Has Grams's house burned down?" Alice asked.

Pop shook his head. "I don't think she's badly hurt, and no, Alice, her house hasn't burned down. Apparently she had a fire in the kitchen and she tried to put it out herself." He turned and looked at the twins. "Which was a very naughty thing for your grandmother to do. What have we told you if there's a fire in the house?"

"Get out!" the twins said in unison.

"Very good. Anyway, she brought in the garden hose—I'm not sure how she managed that—and with all the water she got on the floor, and she admits she was pretty rattled, she slipped and hurt her wrist. Fortunately, a neighbor saw the smoke and called the fire department. Her wrist is badly sprained, and she's not supposed to use it for a while. The doctors put it into a sling."

"What are you going to do?" Ma asked.

"Go and get her. I guess I'll have to bring her here."

Ma swallowed hard. "Where here?" she finally asked.

"Maybe Grams could sleep on the couch," I suggested.

"She can sleep in my bed," Molly said. "I'll sleep on the couch." She smirked at me as if to say I was being selfish by not offering Grams my bed.

"Hey!" I said. "I didn't think Grams would want to share my bed with Daisy."

"She can sleep in our room," Anne said. "I'll let her have the top bunk."

"How long will she be here?" Ma asked. "I mean, a night is

36

one thing. She could sleep in our room for one night, and we can put sleeping bags on the floor of the living room."

Pop started rummaging through his pockets for his car keys. "I don't know. I guess it depends on how much damage was done to her house, and how handicapped she is with her wrist. It may be weeks."

"Your mother would never be happy here, she'd go crazy, she's used to having tons of room," Ma said.

Pop looked at his watch. "I'm sure everything will sort itself out. I've got to go: she's waiting at the hospital. Which one of you kids have my car keys?"

"Why would we have your car keys?" Molly said. "Only Dennie has a license, and she never gets the car."

"You kids are always taking my things," Pop said.

"I can't believe they aren't keeping her overnight," Ma continued to argue. "After all, she's nearly seventy-five. You'd think the hospital would want to observe her."

"Medicare and her insurance won't pay for it," Pop said.

Before Ma could say anything, Pop raised his hand. "I know, I know. It's not fair, but I'm not going to take on city hall tonight. Where are my keys?"

"Right here." Ma picked them up off the counter. They had been behind the salt shaker. "I guess I'd better change the sheets on our bed."

"I thought maybe you could go with me. Make her feel welcome."

Ma nodded. She turned to Dennie. "You and Molly change the sheets and tidy up our bedroom. Andy, see if you can find our sleeping bags. They should be in the garage. And by the way"—she turned as she was almost out of the door—"don't forget that schedule."

After they had gone, Molly started giggling. "Can't you

imagine Grams waiting to get into the bathroom? 'My word, this bathroom is the size of a closet. How do you live like this?' " Dennie and I laughed. Molly's imitation of Grams was pretty good.

But I had the feeling it wasn't really very funny.

DENNIE AND MOLLY AND I DID SIT DOWN AND TRY
to come to some kind of agreement about our schedules, but
it was hard to concentrate.

"Where will Grams sleep if she stays more than a night?"
Molly wondered.

"If Pop has to spend more than a night in a sleeping bag,"
I said, "we're in big trouble."

"She's not going to like us slopping around in sweats,"
Dennie said.

We did finally manage to sort out the baby-sitting chores
for the rest of the week. Then we joined the twins in the living
room. They were watching TV.

"They should be in bed," Dennie said.

"No, no," Anne said. "We want to see Grams and tell her
how much we love her."

Molly shrugged. "Let them stay."

Around ten, we heard our car. I opened the front door and saw Ma and Pop helping Grams up the stairs. Her coat was wrapped around her shoulder and one of her arms was in a sling. She was leaning on Pop while Ma supported her from the back.

Grams is not a short, dumpy grandmother, the kind that bakes cookies and reads stories to the grandkids. She's tall and thin and wears mostly wool slacks and blouses of some shiny material. Even though her hair is gray, from the back she doesn't look old at all. She is bossy, though; she thinks she's always right. Not just about things that she might be right about, like art. She and Grandfather turned part of their Victorian home into an art gallery, so she knows a lot about that. But she gives her opinion on things that Ma says are none of her business, such as whether the twins should wear canvas sneakers all the time, or whether Dennie should be allowed to have a steady boyfriend.

She drives Ma crazy, but I like her. She slips me money and then winks and says, "Don't tell the girls, but I know boys always need more money."

When Grams got to the top of the stairs, she said to me, "Isn't this a fine mess? Here, Andy, be a love and take my purse. Stop pushing me, Elizabeth"—she turned toward Ma—"or I'll fall down again."

I took her purse and laid it on the phone table.

"Where do you want to go?" Pop asked her.

"Go? Go? Home if the truth were known, but since I'm sure you weren't giving me a choice, I guess, wherever you found a corner I can rest my weary bones."

"Does it hurt, Grams?" Anne said.

"How sweet of you to ask." Grams smiled. "Not intolerably.

Brush your bangs out of your eyes, dear; how can you see through all that hair? Do you know that can make you cross-eyed?"

"Dogs have hair that hangs in their eyes and they can see," Anne said. "Daisy's hair hangs in her eyes and she never bumps into anything."

"Her eyes aren't crossed either," Alice added.

"You're not a dog," Grams said. "I'm sure their eyes are made differently or they don't focus the same. I think they see by smelling."

"Alice, Anne, go to bed immediately," Pop yelled. "Do you know what time it is? This is a school night."

"Don't raise your voice with the children," Grams said. "It gets them in the habit of yelling back."

Molly scooped up Anne and carried her down the hallway. Alice followed.

When Ma and Pop, supporting Grams, got to the door of their bedroom, Grams stopped. "Are you actually giving me your room?" she asked. "This is ridiculous. Really, Elizabeth, be sensible. Christopher needs his rest. I can't take his bed. I suppose you'll be sleeping on the couch, or someplace equally uncomfortable. I wouldn't rest a minute knowing you were tossing and turning."

"Please, Mother," Pop said. "Everything's arranged."

"Well, it is your house," Grams conceded. "And I don't want to be a bother. Andy, could you bring in my little suitcase? I think your father put it in the back of the car. You did remember to put in my cosmetic case, Elizabeth?"

"Cosmetic case?" Dennie asked.

"Of course, dear; a woman should always be prepared." She glanced around the room. "It is small, isn't it?"

41

"I'll make you a cup of tea," Ma said.

"That would be nice." Grams sank down on the bed. "But I prefer coffee. Do you have any decaf?"

"Dennie," Pop said, "why don't you help Grams get ready for bed?" He nodded at me. "Andy, get Grams's suitcase." He handed me the keys to the car.

When I woke up the next morning, I heard Ma and Pop whispering. I could tell they were trying to be quiet, but it's hard to fight and keep your voice low at the same time. Daisy began whimpering and pawing at the door.

I let Daisy out. "Sorry," I said.

"That's okay." Ma smiled at me. "She expects a walk at this time since Dennie and I have been taking her jogging."

"I'll take her," I said. I'd rather run Daisy around the block a few times than get involved in whatever they were discussing.

"Fine," Pop said. He turned back to Ma. "I don't mind taking a day off from work, but I think Mother will need help getting dressed and things like that. I'm sure she'd be less embarrassed if you were home to do those things."

I sat on the end of my bed tying my shoes, waiting to see what would happen next. When there was a pause in the argument, I decided it was safe to go out. I shook Daisy's leash at her. She went into her usual frenzy of woofing and leaping and running around in circles. I snapped the leash onto her collar.

"See ya," I said.

Pop nodded.

When I got back, Pop was gone and Ma had changed into jeans and a sweatshirt. She was setting the kitchen table with a ruffled place mat. The orange juice was in a pitcher I had never seen before.

"Wow!" Dennie said, coming into the kitchen. "Pretty fancy. All for us?"

"Dream on," Ma said. "And don't touch that pitcher."

Dennie grabbed a banana from a bowl and leaned against the sink, eating it. "So Dad won and you have to stay home? Where is it written that man's work is more important than woman's?"

"Oh, please," Ma said. "No women's lib this early in the morning. In theory, that's all well and good, but, in practice, when I'm making as much money as your father, then my job will be as important as his."

Molly and the twins came running into the kitchen.

"Sh," Ma whispered. "You'll wake Grams."

I guess Dennie realized the bathroom was probably empty, because she disappeared.

"Since you're home today, does that mean we don't have to worry about the twins?" I asked.

Ma shook her head. "Yes, Andy, I'll be here for the twins. No, Andy, you won't have to come home early. Honestly," she said to no one in particular, "you'd think I was asking you children to do something really hard."

"It's not that," I started to say, but since I couldn't think of what that was, I grabbed my jacket off the kitchen chair and picked up my books. "Are you going with me?" I said to Molly.

"Did you eat anything?" Ma asked me.

I grabbed a banana from the bowl.

"Just wait a minute," Molly said. "Dennie has the bathroom, and I have to brush my teeth."

43

"I'm leaving."

"Andy," Ma said, "grow up."

Molly wandered out of the kitchen, but in a minute she was back. "Where's my jacket?"

"Wherever you put it last," Ma said. "Here." She handed Molly a banana. "Now get out, both of you." Ma didn't raise her voice, but she didn't have to. We can always tell when her patience is giving out.

"Right." I reached out and grabbed Molly around the arm. "Move it," I said.

When we got outside, she turned to me. "Wow! Is Mom going to stay this mad all the time Grams is here?"

"I sure hope not." I couldn't understand why having Grams made Ma so cross.

When I got home from school, Grams was sitting in the kitchen. She looked better than she had the night before. She was even wearing a necklace and large white earrings. The only effect of the fall seemed to be the sling she was wearing on her right arm.

"Well, aren't you early," Ma said sarcastically when she saw me.

"Andy!" Grams exclaimed. "Did you have a good day at school?" She turned toward Molly, who had followed me in. "My, is that the uniform you girls have to wear? I wonder why they picked such a putrid shade of green. It's such an unbecoming color."

Molly looked a little surprised.

"Check and see what the twins are doing." Ma gave Molly a push. "They're supposed to be cleaning their room."

"Do you feel better?" I asked.

"I'm fine," Grams said. "Such foolishness, your mother staying home from work. I can manage just fine."

After dinner, Pop took Grams to see her house. Molly and I decided to go with them.

The outside of Grams's house didn't look so bad. There were greasy smoke stains around some of the windows, and one of the panes of glass was broken, but once we opened the door and went into the hallway, it was obvious that the fire had done a lot of damage.

"Oh, my," Grams said. "I thought it was just in the kitchen." She went into what had once been her living room but had been converted into the art gallery. She walked slowly around. "What happened to all the paintings?" she asked Pop.

"Vivian came over and took them. It's a good thing you have such a loyal salesperson."

"Vivian is more than a salesperson," Grams said. "She's my friend. Were the paintings damaged?"

"Vivian says things weren't a total loss, mostly smoke damage. She said she'd phone you when you're feeling stronger to see about having them cleaned." Pop looked around. "I didn't realize there was so much damage," he said. "Last night we went straight upstairs to get your things, so I didn't have a chance to see much. Don't worry, I'm sure your insurance will cover everything."

"It stinks in here." Molly fanned the air in front of her face. Pop nudged her.

"Well, it does," Molly said, but she shut her mouth.

Grams wasn't paying any attention to us. She wandered over and fingered one of the drapes at the window. When she took her hand away, it was covered with black soot. "It's all gone." She turned toward Pop. "Did you know your father planned this gallery? He even picked out the material for those drapes. He said they should look rich but shouldn't take away from the art. He drove the decorators crazy. 'Subtle, the color must be subtle,' he kept saying to them. He loved this place so. It was his dream."

Pop put his arm around her. "It looks worse than it really is," he said. "We'll get it fixed. Soap and water and a little paint."

"Oh, I don't know." Grams shook her head. "I think I'm too old to start over."

Suddenly she did look old. She even appeared shorter. She had wrinkles I had never noticed before. She almost shuffled out of the gallery and down the hall to the kitchen. We trailed behind her.

The kitchen was a mess. The cabinet doors hung open, the vinyl tiles on the floor had buckled and were curling up, the window over the sink was broken, and all the walls were smeared with black streaks.

"I have to sit down," Grams said.

Pop picked up one of the kitchen chairs, only to discover the legs were charred at the bottom. He started to pick up another chair.

"Oh, don't bother." Grams put her hand on his arm. "I can't stay in here a minute longer." She went back to the hallway and sat down on the stairs. "I feel so helpless."

"It'll be all right." Molly sat down beside her. "My friend Beth had a fire at her house, and her family had to move out for a couple of months. Now you can't even tell there was one."

"I'll get the rest of your clothes." Pop went around Grams and up the stairs.

Grams was sniffling into her handkerchief. Molly kept patting her on the shoulder. I didn't know what to say or do, so I just sat there next to them on the stairs. When Pop called me, I went upstairs to help him carry the suitcases down.

"It's not bad upstairs," Pop said to Grams as he passed her. "You'll probably have to paint and have the drapes cleaned to get the smoke smell out, but basically, nothing has been damaged. I'll get a contractor out here as soon as I can to see what it will cost. Vivian said she can store the paintings."

"I know the carpenter I want, I just can't think of his name right now," Grams said. "I feel so stupid—I've known him for years. My mind seems to have turned to mush. Never mind, we can't do anything tonight. Maybe by tomorrow I'll remember his name. But all this could take months, and I have no place to stay."

"Don't be silly, Mother. You'll stay with us."

"You're a good son, but we'll be at each other's throats in that tiny house." She raised her hand. "No, no, don't argue with me, it's true. Besides, I drive Elizabeth crazy."

I glanced over at Molly and she made a face. I was surprised Grams realized how Ma felt.

"Elizabeth loves you as much as I do," Pop said. "Besides, now that she's working, it will be a big help for you to be there. And the kids love you."

Molly and I nodded our heads.

"I shouldn't let you tempt me. Well, I guess for now I'll stay. If it's too dreadful, I can move into a hotel or something." She straightened the sling on her arm. "As long as I don't have to go to one of those awful old people's homes, I suppose I can stand anything."

THE NEXT DAY WHEN I GOT IN FROM SCHOOL, I almost broke my leg tripping over a stack of what felt like chairs. There's not much light in the garage, but usually I don't need much, since it's a clear shot from the entrance to the stairs. I backed away from the obstacle and looked around. As my eyes got used to the dark, I could make out the china cabinet, the buffet, the dining room table, and the chairs I had fallen over.

Now what, I muttered to myself as I inched my way around the buffet to get to the stairs. When I got to my room, I discovered my bed and bureau were gone!

"Andy, is that you?" Pop came through the kitchen door. He had on his grubby jeans and old sweatshirt.

"What are you doing home from work?" I asked.

"There were things I had to do," Pop said.

"By the way, where're my bed and bureau?"

Pop leaned against the wall and wiped his forehead. "In the kitchen. I thought it would be easier to drag the furniture through your room and down the stairs than to take it out the front door and bring it in through the garage."

"You took all that stuff down the stairs yourself?" I asked.

"No, of course not, I'm not completely crazy. That Murphy boy across the street, the one who goes to San Francisco State, and his friend agreed, for a princely amount, I might add, to move the heavier stuff. They left a few minutes ago. I need you to help me move the living room furniture into the dining room."

"Why?" I followed Pop into the kitchen. I saw my bed and bureau next to the refrigerator. Grams was standing at the stove. "Andy, come here and give me a kiss. I'm glad you're home. Your father has been working himself into a coronary. Honestly, Christopher, this isn't necessary. I could go to a motel or something. Maybe I could stay with Vivian. Of course, she is hard to take. She talks, talks, talks. I think that comes from living alone too long."

"This has all been decided." Pop's voice had that overly patient tone it gets when the twins won't shut up. "Vivian must have a dozen cats, and you know how allergic you are to cats."

"She only has three," Grams said. She wrestled with a saucepan before she put it back on the stove. "Andy, lift this pot for me. I never realized how much a person needs both hands."

"Mother, will you get away from the stove. Next you'll scald yourself."

"Now, don't fuss, Christopher. I'm not a complete invalid.

49

I was fixing a cup of coffee. I couldn't find a kettle." She glanced around the kitchen. "It must be somewhere. Every kitchen has a kettle."

"I think it melted last week," I said. Ma was always burning up kettles. When Dennie asked her what she was going to buy with her first paycheck, Ma had said, "I'd like a microwave oven. I understand water boils so fast you don't have time to forget it." So far, though, she hadn't bought one.

Grams started to say something, but Pop pushed her into a chair, poured the boiling water from the pot into a mug, and set it on the table in front of her. He got the jar of instant coffee and a spoon. "Now, you just sit there and relax," he said.

"You don't have to wait on me, Christopher. My goodness. I never realized how handy you are in the kitchen. Your father wouldn't have recognized the stove if it burned him. Of course, men weren't expected to do women's work in those days."

Pop didn't answer. He steered me through the dining room, which now held the couch and two chairs from the living room.

"I figured that your mother and I would use the living room as our bedroom and we'd use the dining room as the living room. Grams can have our room. It seemed to your mother and me that the dining room was more expendable than the living room. We'll just eat in the kitchen."

I nodded. It sounded good to me. The number of times we ate in the dining room each year could be counted on one hand. I wondered why they hadn't thought of this solution when the twins took my room.

"So." Pop rubbed his hands. "Let's get all these little tables and lamps and things out of here."

50

PROPERTY OF
FRANKFORT HIGH SCHOOL

"Right," I said. "But what are you and Ma going to do for a bed and stuff?"

"I phoned one of those furniture rental places, and they're delivering a complete bedroom set tomorrow morning."

Grams wandered in from the kitchen. "Did they sterilize the mattress?" she asked.

"It's the law," Pop said through clenched teeth.

"I should certainly hope so." Grams shook her head. "What will we do about Thanksgiving?"

Pop indicated I was to take one end of a lamp table. We started to maneuver it through the door. "What about Thanksgiving?" he said.

"Where will we eat it? I mean, you won't have a dining room anymore."

"I don't think that's a serious problem," Pop said. "We can eat in the kitchen or in a restaurant. Be careful going through the door."

"Thanksgiving in a restaurant! That's so tacky. Only people who have no family or friends or a home eat in restaurants on Thanksgiving," Grams said.

Pop started to laugh. He put down his end of the table. "That is the most ridiculous thing I ever heard. People who have money to pay someone else to cook their turkeys eat in restaurants. When is Thanksgiving, anyway?"

"Two weeks," Grams said. "Are Elizabeth's parents coming?"

"Probably," Pop said.

Grandma and Grandpa Reid live in Los Angeles. Actually, since Grandpa retired, they really live in their motor home. They belong to some kind of club where everybody has a motor home and they meet at campgrounds in different states

51

and have barbecues and stuff. When they're not doing that, they visit Ma's brother Uncle Vince and his family in Arizona or Ma's other brother, Uncle Andrew, in Oregon. Except for the big holidays, Thanksgiving, Christmas, and Easter, we never know when they're going to show up.

Grandma and Grandpa are completely different from Grams. Grandma is short and chubby. Dennie once told her that if she exercised and ate more salads, she could lose weight and look much better. Grandma didn't get mad. She just laughed and said, "Honey, when you get to be my age, the only people who pay any attention to you are old men and kids. I'm not going to make myself miserable for some old man, and kids like me the way I am. Besides, a little bit of padding keeps you from getting wrinkles." And when Dennie mentioned to her that polyester was out and natural fibers were in, Grandma said they might be in for people who live in a house, but if you live in a trailer, polyester is the only practical material, since, like her face, it doesn't wrinkle. I have to admit that she doesn't seem to have many wrinkles.

"I guess they'll be sleeping in that dreadful motor home?" Grams asked. "I can't understand how they can. I would feel as if I were living in the back seat of a car." She wandered into the kitchen, but then she came to the dining room door. "I was thinking," she said, "why don't you and Elizabeth move into the dining room, and that would save you from changing the living room?"

Pop and I were now carrying the TV set. He waited until we positioned it in a corner before he answered. "Liz and I thought of that," he said. "But since the kids often use the kitchen table to do their homework, it just seemed we would get more privacy if we weren't sleeping next to the kitchen."

Grams sighed and then she asked, "Shouldn't Molly and the twins be home?"

"Molly's over at Cherry Garden Convalescent Hospital," I said. "She'll be home around five-thirty."

"Is it safe for her to be out alone at this hour? It's getting really dark."

"She gets a ride home from one of her friend's mothers," I said.

"Maybe I can do something about dinner?" Grams suggested. "Did Elizabeth leave anything?"

Pop frowned. He was standing in front of the TV with the electric cord in one hand and the cable box in the other. "I plugged in the set and all I got was snow," he said.

"That's because the dining room isn't wired for cable and we got rid of the antenna," I said.

"What do you mean?" Pop asked me.

"That we won't get very good reception until we have the dining room wired for cable."

Pop muttered an obscenity under his breath before asking, "Who should I call?"

"The cable company. Do you want me to do it for you?"

"I'd see if there was anything in the refrigerator for dinner, but I can't get the door open." Grams was still talking. "Andy's bureau is in the way."

Pop looked up. "I'm sure Liz has taken care of dinner."

"If Molly's at that Cherry Garden place, where are the twins? It's almost six," Grams said.

Actually it still wasn't even five-thirty. "Dennie and Bruce picked them up. Maybe they went for a ride or something," I said.

"What time do you usually eat dinner?" Grams asked.

"Mother, please," Pop said. "Don't worry. We will have dinner tonight."

"You don't have to shout," Grams said. "I'm just trying to be helpful." She turned and left the dining room. In a minute I heard the door to her bedroom quietly close. I looked at Pop. He made a face. "Phone the cable company," he said.

We had just finished setting up my room again when Ma got home. She had stopped at the store and bought a couple of precooked chickens.

"Thank God," Pop said. "My mother was convinced we were going to starve."

Ma shoved the chickens into the oven and pulled a pot off the rack. "Where are the twins? I can use them to set the table."

"Dennie and Bruce have them," I said.

"Chris, why don't you take a nice shower. You must be exhausted, moving all that furniture," Ma said.

By six-thirty, everybody had gotten home, and Ma had dinner on the table. Pop went off to get Grams. We could hear him say softly, "Mother, dinner's ready." She must have answered him, because after a minute we heard him say, "Now, Mother, don't be foolish. You must be hungry and we're all waiting for you."

After a few minutes, Pop and Grams appeared in the kitchen.

Ma jumped to her feet. "Sit down, Grams," she said. "We waited for you."

I expected Grams to say something, but she didn't. She sat quietly at the table. The rest of us were so busy eating everything in sight that it wasn't until Dennie started to pick up the plates that we noticed Grams hadn't eaten anything.

"Don't you feel well?" Pop asked. "Is your wrist bothering you?"

"Now, don't worry about me, I'm fine." Grams tried to smile, but all she managed was a slight change in her expression. "I guess I'm just a little tired. I'm not used to so much confusion."

"Now that we've gotten all the furniture moved around, things will be much quieter for you," Pop said.

"What time is that furniture coming tomorrow?" Ma left the table and began opening a can of fruit cocktail.

"I couldn't get a firm time out of them," Pop said. "I couldn't even get them to say if it would be morning or afternoon."

"Maybe I could call them tomorrow when I get to work, and then, if they have a delivery time, I can run home for a few minutes to let them in."

"I would stay, but there's that big meeting I have to go to," Pop said.

"I'll stay home," I said.

"Why should he get to stay home?" Molly demanded. She frowned at me. "I bet you have a test tomorrow."

"Please." Grams raised her good hand. "I'll be here all day. I can certainly open the door and let the delivery people in. Just tell me where you want things and I'll be sure they put the furniture in the right place."

"Well," said Pop, "if you wouldn't mind. I'll leave a check for the first month's payment."

"No," Grams said. "I want to pay. After all, you wouldn't need to use someone else's things if I weren't here."

"Since Grams is going to be here, can we come home after school?" Anne asked. "I don't want to go over to Susie's anymore. She's mean. She won't let us play with her toys, and she bit Alice."

"She bit Alice?" Ma asked. "Where?"

"Here." Alice extended her arm.

55

Pop examined the two black-and-blue marks. "It doesn't look like the skin was broken."

"Why would Susie bite you?" Ma asked.

"I don't know," Alice said.

We all looked at Anne.

"I don't know," Anne said.

"Well, you don't have to worry anymore," Grams suddenly said. "All this fussing about who watches Alice and Anne. If I'm going to be here, I might as well make myself useful." She patted Alice's arm. "Grams is here, and she won't let anything happen to you." She smiled at the rest of us. "That solves that problem."

"That's very nice of you," Ma said. "Except it's more complicated. Chris drops them off in the morning, but someone has to pick them up after school. They're too little to come home alone."

"Before you started to work, how did they get home?" Grams asked.

"Actually, it was only for a couple of weeks," Ma said. "I walked over and got them. But it's five blocks each way."

Grams nodded. "I'll take a cab," she said.

"A cab!" Pop repeated. "That would cost a fortune."

"It couldn't be that expensive. I can afford it, and it won't be for long. I'm sure the doctor will let me drive again very soon." She turned to Pop. "I was thinking. There's no sense in letting my car sit in the garage at home. In fact, it probably isn't very safe there. It's obvious the house is empty and being worked on, so somebody could decide to steal it. Dennie and Bruce could drive over after school and bring it here." She smiled at Dennie. "And when I'm not using it, Dennie would be free to use it. She can drive Molly and Andy to school.

Then Molly would be perfectly safe and Andy won't have to worry about her."

"Grams!" Dennie squealed. "That's wonderful."

"My pleasure," Grams said.

Ma started to say something, but Pop raised an eyebrow and shook his head slightly. "Why don't you show Grams where you want the bedroom furniture to go. The kids and I'll clean up the kitchen," he said. Then he looked at me. "What did the cable company say?"

"The place was closed. I'll call tomorrow."

"I can't believe I'll have a car to drive to school," Dennie said. "This is great."

"I always worried about you and Molly on those public buses," Grams said.

"Oh, honestly!" Ma exclaimed.

I wondered why she looked so angry. It seemed to me that all her problems had been solved.

GRAMS NOT ONLY TOOK OVER WATCHING THE twins but, even with her sling, started cooking dinner every night. This only left the laundry and cleaning for Dennie, Molly, and me to argue about. I would have thought Ma'd love to come home and have dinner ready, but she didn't. She kept trying to control the meals. In the morning before she left for work, Ma would say things like, "I left the meat or the casserole out to thaw." Grams would smile and nod and then proceed to fix something else, mostly stuff she claimed Pop liked when he was little. When Ma came home she would sniff and say, "That doesn't smell like tamale pie" or whatever she had left.

Then Grams would say, "Now, you just sit down, you've been working hard all day. I don't know how you do it. I'll dish up dinner."

At first Ma wouldn't give in. She would look at her plate and ask, "What happened to the tamale pie?"

Grams would say, "I put it back in the freezer. I thought we'd have bifteck sauté à la bordelaise. Now, don't worry about the cost, I paid for the ingredients."

After a week of this game, Ma stopped asking questions, and she ate whatever Grams was serving without making comments. Other things had changed, too. For one thing, Grams now sat in Ma's chair. I realize she took that chair because it was closest to the stove, so it was easier to serve the food, but now Ma sat in the chair that people like Bruce used. Ma had become a kind of guest.

I have to admit that some of the meals Grams served were different, to say the least. Once Dennie took a bite of a strange-looking vegetable and asked, "Dad, did you really like this stuff when you were a kid?"

"Of course he didn't," Ma said. But she spoke so low I don't think Grams could hear her.

Pop made sure Grams was busy at the stove before he said, "It tastes different now."

"I'm glad to hear you admit it," Ma said. "I'd hate to think you find this stuff edible."

Pop glanced back and saw that Grams was starting toward the table. "Oh, it's not that bad," he said and quickly shoveled a forkful into his mouth. That seemed to make Ma mad because she suddenly put her fork down and started to clear the table.

On Thanksgiving, Grandma and Grandpa Reid drove their motor home up from Los Angeles, Grandpa honking the last block to let us know they had arrived.

Ma rolled her eyes. "My father is too much," she said to Grams.

"I never could understand the male propensity for making noise," Grams said.

As far as I'm concerned, Thanksgiving, aside from the sports on TV, is pretty much of a nothing. Turkey and dressing are not my favorite foods. Usually Ma and Grandma did the meal and Grams and her friend Vivian came over as guests. This year, Vivian didn't come, and Grams acted as if it was her kitchen and Ma and Grandma were the guests.

"Don't bother about the stuffing," she told Ma. "I've got this interesting recipe. When Anthony was alive, we once spent Thanksgiving in Paris. Of course, they don't have Thanksgiving, but a darling little couple made us this simply fabulous oyster and truffle and rice dressing." She turned to Grandpa Reid. "You and Ethel should really go over to Europe. It's such an enlarging experience."

Grandma laughed. "Really, Louise, I think I'm large enough. That dressing sounds awfully rich, and where in the world did you get truffles?"

"Aren't those the things pigs sniff out?" Grandpa asked. Then he started snuffling and chasing the twins all over the house.

"I didn't get truffles, they're prohibitively expensive, but I found this Japanese mushroom I thought I could substitute."

"That seems an awful waste," Ma said. "I've already made the dressing. I was just about to stuff the bird."

"Just as well," said Grandma Reid. "I don't think Bill, or Chris, for that matter, should eat anything so rich. We'd better stick with our regular bread stuffing."

"Honestly." Grams looked at both Ma and Grandma and then she left the kitchen. When Grams was out of hearing, Ma said, "She goes off to her room for the least little thing." They both started to laugh.

I went into the living room to watch the football game. I didn't think anything was very funny.

When we were ready to sit down for dinner, Grams was still in her room.

"If you ask me," Grandma Reid said, "someone is sulking."

"I'm not sulking, Grandma," Anne said. "Look, I'm smiling so hard you can see my teeth."

"There's a thief in this house," Grandpa shouted. "Alice, Anne, why didn't you tell me?"

"What? Where?" squealed Anne.

"What did they steal?" Alice looked under the table.

"Two front teeth," Grandpa roared. "Somebody stole your teeth."

Alice and Anne burst out laughing, showing the space where their teeth had been.

"They fell out, Grandpa, and the Tooth Fairy gave us two quarters each. Anne lost her tooth first, and mine fell out the next day," Alice said.

"Fell out?" Grandpa raised his hands up in surprise. "That's terrible. You poor things. Has anything else fallen out? Are all your fingers and toes still in place? Maybe your hair is falling out and you'll look like me." He leaned over and gave a tug to Alice's hair. "Is your hair loose?"

By this time the twins were shouting and pulling at each other's hair.

"Now see what you've done," Grandma said. "You're getting them all excited."

"You two." Ma looked at the twins. "Just settle down. Chris, why don't you go and get Grams? She's in her room."

Pop went off, and pretty soon he and Grams came back to the kitchen.

"Almost ate the turkey without you," Grandpa said. He had been carving the bird. "Here, hand me your plate. As I remember, you're a white-meat person?"

Grams nodded.

We were almost finished when the phone rang. Dennie leaped up to answer it. She was back in a minute. "That was Bruce. He wondered if I could go over to his house for dessert?"

Ma sighed. "I guess so," she said. "Is he coming over right away?"

"Not exactly," Dennie said. "His brother took the car over to his girlfriend's. Grams, would you mind awfully if I took your car?"

"Is it safe for you to be out so late?" Grandma Reid asked.

"Tell you what, pumpkin," Grandpa said, "I'll drive you over in the motor home. That should impress your boyfriend."

"Now, Bill," Grandma said. "You've had a glass of wine."

"You're not going to be late, are you?" Pop asked.

Grandma Reid said, "My goodness. Is it nice for girls to go over to boys' houses just like that?"

"I thought the same thing," Grams said. "But I was told I was old-fashioned. We have to move with the times."

"Are you a good driver, dear?" Grandma asked.

"Of course she is," Grams said. "I let her take my car to school every day. I must admit, though, I'll be glad to drive again. I miss being independent."

"Will you need that sling for much longer?" Grandma asked.

"No, the wrist doesn't bother me at all. I expect when I see the doctor next week, he'll let me take it off."

Dennie wouldn't like that, I thought. Actually, it had been

handy getting a ride to school every day, although, in spite of what Grams said, I didn't think Dennie was such a good driver.

On the Monday morning after Thanksgiving, as Molly got into Grams's car, she asked, "Dennie? What do you think Grams would say if I asked her to visit Cherry Garden? I have this great idea for a report about an old person visiting a convalescent hospital."

I climbed into the back. "Why would Grams want to do something as stupid as that?" I asked. "She's plenty busy doing Ma's job."

"Honestly, Andy, you are the most insensitive person I have ever met," Dennie said.

"Insensitive? What do you mean, insensitive? All I said was why would she want to go visit a bunch of old people?"

Dennie ignored me. "I think it's a great idea." She looked at Molly. "Grams needs friends her own age to talk to."

"How am I insensitive?" I asked again. "And will you please look where you're driving."

Dennie faced forward. "You have no idea what's going on," she said.

"I don't know what you're talking about," I said.

"Of course you don't—that's just the point." Dennie slowed the car down for a red light. She looked at Molly. "I bet Mom would love to have her develop other interests."

"That too," said Molly. "But I thought I could get a report out of how an older person feels visiting a place like Cherry Garden. Maybe I could even use the subject for my final paper. Besides, it seems to me, the patients would rather have people their own age visiting them."

"Why isn't Ma happy that Grams takes care of the twins?" I said. "I would think that it solves her problems."

"Mom wants to solve her own problems," Dennie said to me. "You know, Molly, the idea gets better the more I think about it. Maybe Grams could come and visit my death and dying class."

The light changed and Dennie took her foot off the brake and put it on the gas pedal. She almost hit a dog who had decided to cross the street. She braked so hard my books and papers tumbled to the floor. That's a good example of why I always rode in the back seat. There was a gentle bump from behind.

"What was that?" Dennie squealed. "Did somebody hit us?"

"I think they just nudged us," I said. "You did stop too suddenly."

"What was I supposed to do, hit that dog?"

"If you hadn't been so busy talking and looking around, you would have seen the dog," I said.

Dennie scowled and leaned her head out the window. The cars behind us were starting to honk.

"What'll I do?" she asked.

"I didn't hear anything break," I said. "I doubt if there's any damage. These old cars are pretty indestructible. I'd just drive on. The guy who hit us is gone."

"Okay," Dennie said, but she didn't sound convinced. She drove slowly down the street. When another car honked at her, she almost jumped a foot. "Now what did I do?" she asked. "Why is that person honking at me?"

"I think you're going too slow," I said.

"Oh, for heaven's sake, what's their hurry?"

We finally arrived at Bishop Alemany. Dennie pulled into a parking space as far away from everyone else as she could. We got out of the car and Dennie went to look at the back of the car. Molly and I followed her. "I don't see a dent," Dennie said.

I barely glanced at the car. "It wasn't hit hard enough to do any damage," I said.

Molly ran her finger along the metal trim. "I can't feel anything."

"Even if there was a scratch, Grams will never notice," I added.

Later that morning, I was putting away my books and searching for my lunch when I heard somebody shouting my name. I looked up. Karen was standing in front of me.

"Hey, Andy, I want to talk to you."

"Okay," I said. "But I don't need any more baby-sitting."

She took a deep breath. "I'm giving a party next Saturday night, and I was wondering if you'd like to come?"

I stalled, racking my brain and trying to think of a good excuse, any excuse. What would make her think I'd want to go to a party at her house? "I'm not sure," I finally said. "Can I get back to you?"

"Sure, Andy." She stood there shifting her books from one arm to the other. "It's just a bunch of kids, nothing special."

I nodded.

"So." She kept smiling. "You'll let me know?"

"Right." I looked at her and she looked at me. I would have left, but I needed to get my lunch out of my locker.

"I'll be hearing from you?" She backed up a few feet.

At this rate we'd still be staring at each other when the bell rang and lunchtime was over. "Is there something else?" I finally asked.

"No," she said. "Well." She backed up a few more feet. "So long."

"Right," I said again. I turned to my locker.

Why did I do that, I asked myself. I should have said no right off. Now I'd have to get in touch with her to let her know

I couldn't go. Then I realized I could write her a note and shove it into her locker.

I grabbed my lunch bag and went to look for Martin. It was one of those late fall days in San Francisco when the sky is clear of fog and the sun is shining and it's warmer than it is during the summer. Most of the school were eating lunch outside. I was shocked to find Martin talking to Molly! Probably she was asking him if he thought it was a good idea to ask Grams to visit Cherry Garden. I went up to them.

"Get lost," I said to her.

She blushed.

"It's okay," Martin said to her. "I think it's a great idea."

"Thanks." Molly gave me a dirty look and left.

"Was she bothering you?"

"No," Martin said. "She was just asking about the sort of oral reports Ms. Jackson wants and whether I thought Ms. Jackson would allow her to write about her grandmother. Molly's not so bad."

"Come on, she's a little kid," I replied.

"She's almost Jennie's age," Martin said, referring to his freshman sister. "And Jennie's convinced my parents she should be able to date. I can't imagine anybody asking her out, though."

I shrugged and watched Molly walk across the campus. I couldn't imagine anybody asking her for a date, either.

It was almost as if Molly had heard my conversation with Martin, because at dinner that night she brought up the Winter Mixer. Molly really should have negotiated the dance in private, but I guess she figured that maybe Dennie would offer her support.

"You're much too young to go," Grams said immediately.

Ma looked annoyed.

"I remember when I went to that dance as a freshman," Dennie said. "It was terrible. None of the boys asked me to dance. They just hung around the door and snickered at the girls."

Pop started to say something, but Grams interrupted. "I never really approved of Dennie going out so early, but she was much more mature than Molly is." She looked over at Molly. "Molly still looks like a little girl."

There was a shocked silence around the table. Molly burst into tears.

"Darling." Ma got up and put an arm around Molly. "Don't cry. Grams didn't really mean anything by that."

"Yes she did," Molly said. "Because it's true. I know I look like a little kid in that uniform. I thought Dennie would help me find a dress that would make me look more grownup. I just want to be like the other kids, but even you think I'm just a baby."

"There's nothing wrong with being a late bloomer," Grams said.

"Molly," Dennie said, "don't cry. I can fix you up so you'll look at least fifteen."

"It would take a miracle!" Molly wailed.

"Why is Molly crying?" Anne asked.

"Molly is feeling a little upset," Grams said. "You two eat your dinner or you can't have any dessert, and Grams made you your favorite chocolate pudding."

Molly got up from the table and ran out of the room. Ma got up, too. She gave Pop a nudge as she followed Molly.

"Such a fuss," Grams said, smiling at the rest of us.

Pop cleared his throat. "I think—" he started to say.

"Now, now. Here, have some more to eat." Grams passed him the platter of fried chicken. "Don't pay any attention. She's

67

just having an adolescent tantrum. Andy, pass your father the mashed potatoes."

"Sure," I said.

Pop took the dish I offered him. He stared at it for a minute and then he put it down. Ma came back to the table. She looked angry.

"Is Molly all right?" Pop asked.

"Yes, she's feeling better. I told her you and I would discuss the dance tonight." She emphasized the words "you" and "I." She didn't look at Grams when she said it.

"Fine," Pop said.

"Poor Molly," Dennie said. "I can't think of anything worse than being a freshman. No matter what you do or how you dress, nothing ever seems right. I remember how stupid I felt asking a boy to the Vice Versa Dance."

"I never heard of such a thing," Grams said. "Nice girls don't ask boys for a date."

"It happens all the time," I said. "Some girl asked me to a party just today."

Grams looked shocked.

"Are you going?" Dennie asked.

"Nah," I said. "Karen's a flake."

"I suppose you told her that?" Dennie asked.

"Of course not," I said. "What kind of a clod do you think I am?" Which reminded me, I had to find out Karen's locker number so I could leave her a note turning her down.

IN THE KITCHEN THE NEXT MORNING, DENNIE SAID
to Molly, "Tough luck. Maybe they'll let you go to a dance
next semester."

I was surprised that Molly hadn't convinced Ma and Pop
that she was old enough to go to the dance. I thought Ma
would agree just to show Grams who was the boss.

Molly shrugged. Maybe she hadn't really wanted to go
anyway. She wasn't blaming Grams, though, because she
turned to her and said, "You know, one of my class projects
is to visit Cherry Garden Convalescent Hospital."

"Yes, dear." Grams was busy at the stove making me pancakes.

"I was thinking you might like visiting there sometime?"

"Cherry Garden? Isn't that one of those dreadful rest
homes?" Grams asked.

"Yes," I interrupted. "Stop bothering Grams." I don't want

to sound like a pig or anything, but pancakes are something I was lucky to see twice a year, and having them on a weekday was pretty unbelievable.

"Cherry Garden isn't so bad." Molly frowned at me. "But some of the people there are lonely, and I thought you could be a sort of inspiration, being so independent and having your own business and all."

I was impressed. I didn't know Molly was capable of such a snow job.

Grams turned my pancakes over before she answered Molly. "Why, what a nice thing to say. I suppose, if it would help you and inspire those poor unfortunates, I could visit the place. I see my doctor tomorrow. If he lets me drive, I'd be glad to go."

"Great!" Molly said.

"Sit down, dear, and have some pancakes. Dennie, do you want some?"

"None for me," Dennie said. "I think I should lose a little weight. One of my customers asked me if I ever wore any of the clothes I sell."

"You look fine to me," Grams said. "Your grandfather always said he preferred young ladies with a little meat on them."

Dennie frowned, grabbed a banana from the bowl, and wandered out.

"Good thing she left," I said. "I thought these were my pancakes."

"Now, Andy, there are plenty for all of you." Grams stacked an even number on two plates.

"Well," Molly whispered to me, "that solves the problem of my next report."

"That class sounds like a royal pain." I grabbed the syrup bottle before Molly could.

"It's okay. I like Mr. Simpson, the man I visit. He had a stroke and can't walk, and he's hard to understand, but he plays a mean game of chess. He actually beat me a couple of times. What I hate is giving those reports. Nothing much happens from week to week." She reached over and took the syrup bottle from me. "The paper at the end is a snap. I'm good at writing papers."

I was severely tempted to shove her face into her plate.

When we were on our way to school, Molly said to Dennie, "I just hope Grams'll be able to drive."

"No offense," Dennie replied, "but I'd just as soon she didn't. I like having a car to use."

Grams did get to drive. Vivian took her to her doctor's appointment in Alameda. Pop came home early to watch the twins. It was almost nine that night before Grams got home. She was dressed up and looked excited.

"The doctor said I was just fine," she said as she came into the house. "No problem with driving at all. After I saw him, Vivian and I went over to my house."

"It must be almost finished," Ma said.

"I'm afraid not," Grams replied. "I don't remember Mr. Simpkins being this poky."

"He's not a spring chicken," Pop said.

"Maybe you should get another contractor?" Ma suggested.

"Oh, I couldn't do that," Grams said. "I'd only trust the job to him. Besides, there's no hurry. One month or two, it doesn't really matter."

"I would think Vivian would be anxious to get back to work," Ma said.

"Oh, technically Vivian is still working. She supervised the cleaning of the paintings and she's actually sold some. She's got them stored in her garage. It's funny, she only sees people by appointment, and yet our business is quite good." Grams turned to Molly. "Vivian thought it was a very clever idea of yours, my going to that rest home. She says with the holidays and all, it would be an act of charity. Of course, I won't be able to go with you after school, I have to be home for the twins, but late morning, early afternoon would be a perfect time for me to visit."

"Great!" Molly said. "I'll talk to Mrs. Walsh, who runs Cherry Garden. I'm sure she won't care what time you come."

"Well," Grams said, "I've had a busy day. Good night, all. Oh, Dennie, be sure to leave the car keys for me, and, Molly, don't worry about calling Mrs. Walsh. I think it would be better if I talked to her myself." Grams disappeared down the hallway.

"That's certainly good news," Pop said. Then he looked at Ma. "About her wrist," he added.

The next day Molly and I were back to taking the bus, and Dennie went with Bruce. Grams drove the twins to school to, as she phrased it, save Pop the added job. The coach canceled practice that day, so I ended up getting home early. When I got off the bus, I noticed a police car parking near our house. Grams's car, driven by another policeman, pulled in behind. I started running, and when I got closer, I saw Grams get out of the back of the police car. I sprinted the last couple of yards.

"Grams!" I shouted. "Are you okay? What happened?"

Grams was leaning on the arm of a policeman. Her hat was

on her head crooked, and her coat, half off her shoulder, was trailing on the street.

"Your grandmother was in an accident." The policeman reached down and gathered up the ends of her coat so that she wouldn't trip.

"An accident!" I cried. I looked over at her car. It looked okay to me. "Is the other car wrecked?"

"Really, Andy." Grams made a vague gesture as if to straighten her hat. "A car is a machine. I ran over a human being."

"You killed someone?" I asked in horror.

"It wasn't that bad," the policeman said. "He isn't dead; the paramedic thought he probably had a broken ankle."

The policeman started to steer Grams up the stairs.

I ran ahead and unlocked the front door.

"Are you the only one home?" the policeman asked me.

I nodded and then I looked at my watch. "Grams?" I asked. "Where are the twins?"

"Oh, Lord." Grams stopped in the doorway. "What time is it?"

"Three forty-five," I said. "They've been out of school at least an hour. Maybe I better run down to the school."

"Is there a problem?" the policeman asked. "Can we help?"

"No, no, wait," Grams said. "I must be losing my mind. I remember now. I wasn't sure if I'd be delayed at Cherry Garden, so I made arrangements for them to go home with Susie. I thought I could pick them up there."

"If everything's okay," the policeman said, "we'll be going. You stay here with your grandmother. I don't think she should be alone. Why don't you make her a nice cup of tea?"

"Coffee," Grams muttered.

"Was it her fault?" I asked.

"From what the witnesses said, the man was jaywalking and your grandmother wasn't speeding." The policeman handed Grams's car keys to me. "I think we can call it an accident."

I nodded and closed the front door. Grams was standing by the phone. She was still wearing her hat and coat. "It was terrible," she said. "Terrible, and I didn't hit that poor man once, I hit him twice!"

I stared at her. "Twice?"

She started struggling out of her coat. I took it from her and laid it on the hall chair. She looked a funny gray color, so I thought I had better get her that cup of coffee.

"Didn't you know you hit him?" I asked.

"Of course I knew." She followed me out to the kitchen. "I just got confused. I shifted into drive by mistake." She took off her hat and laid it on the table.

I picked up a pot and started running water into it.

"I'm a menace. I'll never drive again. They should lock me up. Andy, turn off that water, you're wasting it. The pan is overflowing."

"Huh, oh, yeah." I turned off the faucet.

"Here, let me." Grams took the pot out of my hands, put it on the stove, and turned on the electricity. She suddenly said, "What am I doing? I almost killed a man and I'm calmly making myself a cup of coffee."

I wouldn't have exactly described her as calm. "Where did this accident happen?"

"In front of that rest home place, Cherry Fruit or something."

"Garden," I said.

"Whatever. There was this man. I saw him, I really did, but I didn't realize that he was going to cross the street. All of a sudden he was right in front of me and then he fell, just like that, under the car." She tried to snap her fingers but couldn't.

"What did you do then?" I couldn't figure out how she hit him twice.

"I stopped, of course. What do you think I did?"

"Then why . . ." I started to say.

"Everybody was shouting at me. They kept yelling to move the car back, so I did, except the car was in drive and I ran right over him. At least, I think I did—I don't remember anymore. When the policeman started asking me questions and writing things down, for the life of me, I got all confused. He must think I'm senile." She paused to pour the water out of the pot into a cup. She spooned in some coffee and carried the cup to the table, pulled out a chair and sat down, and took a sip. She frowned. "This water isn't even hot. What was I saying?"

"You were telling me what happened."

Grams closed her eyes for a minute. "Everybody was shouting at me." She took another sip of the cold coffee. "I wonder, where do all those strangers come from when there's an accident. There must have been twenty people standing around."

"You actually ran over him again?" I asked.

"Of course not. I stopped the car and got out. Good thing the car wasn't on Mr. Wagner."

"Mr. Wagner?" I said.

"That's the name he gave the police. Do you know a Mr. Wagner?"

"No, but I think my friend Martin visited a man called Mr. Wagner when he had that class last year."

"It must be the same man. He said he lived at Cherry Garden, and I don't imagine there's more than one Mr. Wagner there." She shook her head. "Now it seems worse. I've run over a friend of yours." Grams started to cry.

"Grams?" I said. I had never seen a grownup cry, at least not the way Grams was crying. She had put her head on the table and was sobbing loudly, the way the twins do.

I started to go over to her when the doorbell rang.

When I opened the door, Mrs. Kennedy was there with the twins.

"Oh, good," she said. "You're home. I forgot I have to pick up my mother-in-law at five. I took a chance that someone would be home. Is it okay if I leave them?"

I nodded and thanked her. Anne and Alice went running off in the direction of the kitchen. Anne came back to the hall. "Grams is crying," she said.

"Don't bother her," I said. "Why don't you guys watch TV."

"Is Grams sick?" Anne persisted.

"No." I turned on the TV, found a cartoon show, and then looked into the kitchen. Grams was still sitting at the table, but at least she wasn't sobbing. I cautiously went in.

"I won't bite," Grams said. "Don't look so scared." She sighed. "Why should anybody be scared of me?" She didn't wait for an answer but went on. "I've been thinking. I have to find out how that poor man is. Get me the phone book, dear. What hospital do you think he was taken to?" She seemed to be talking more to herself than to me, so I didn't answer the last question. I went out to the hallway and got the phone book and brought it back to her.

"Maybe I should just phone that Cherry Garden. They must know his condition by now." She got up. "I won't rest until I know the worst. For the life of me, I don't understand what made him suddenly decide to cross the street."

I stayed in the kitchen. I heard the twins talking to Grams as she went through to the hall.

Anne put her head around the door. "Grams smiled at me," she said.

"Is that the news flash of the day?" I said.

"Are you feeling sick now, too?" Anne asked. When I ignored her, she went back into the living room.

After a few minutes, Grams came back. "I feel a little better," she said. "He's at St. Anne's Hospital and he's doing fine. He has a broken ankle. I'll send flowers, of course, but I wonder if I should go visit him and tell him how sorry I am."

"Gee, Grams, do you think that's smart? It's sort of like admitting guilt."

"But I am guilty," she said.

I decided I was out of my depth. I'd let Pop handle it.

Actually, Ma was the one to keep her head. When Pop heard the story, he got almost as pale as Grams had been.

"Are you sure you're okay?" he kept asking. "Why don't you go and lie down?"

Finally Grams said, "Christopher, stop fussing at me. I'm fine."

"I'd feel better if your doctor could look at you," he said.

"I wasn't hit by a car. I hit someone, a Mr. Wagner."

"But the shock . . ." Pop argued.

"I ordered flowers," Grams said. "But I thought I'd visit him tomorrow."

"Mother! You can't do that," Pop said.

"I don't know why she can't," Ma said. "I think it would be very nice of her."

"Are you going to drive to St. Anne's Hospital?" Dennie asked. "Because, I mean, if you're nervous or anything, I could take off from school and drive you."

"Oh." Grams laid her fork down.

77

We were having bacon and eggs for dinner again. Obviously, Grams hadn't cooked dinner.

"You're right. I shouldn't be driving."

"Grams," Dennie said, "I didn't mean that. Why, you've been driving for years and this is your first accident. I didn't mean you couldn't drive, I just thought you might be upset and worried about seeing Mr. Wagner."

"You're sweet," Grams said. "Thank you. I'm sure you're right. Just now, I don't think I could get behind the wheel of a car. I'll take a cab."

"I hope you realize that if you go see this man, it might influence the insurance companies?" Pop said.

"I realize I have to do what is right," Grams said. "I may be getting old, but I haven't lost my sense of values."

"I never said that." Pop stabbed at a piece of bacon.

"Good thing," Grams said. "I'm not senile yet."

She seemed to have recovered from the accident.

"HEY," I SAID TO MARTIN THE NEXT MORNING, "you had to visit a Mr. Wagner at Cherry Garden last year, didn't you?"

"Don't remind me," Martin said. "He was the meanest, crankiest man I ever met. Complain, complain, complain. You should ask Barry. He and his girlfriend, Rory, found him one night when he ran away. Can you imagine, this old guy actually ran away?"

"From Cherry Garden?"

"No, from his daughter's house when she'd had him over for dinner. She was always crying and saying she couldn't understand her father. She said he acts as if he doesn't love her. Sickening. Why do you want to know?"

"My grandmother ran over him yesterday."

Martin almost dropped his books. "You're kidding. Is he dead?"

"No, his ankle is broken. Grams is going over to visit him today at the hospital."

"Well, good luck to her. If he finds out she hit him, he'll probably kill her or sue her. Yeah, that's what he'll do, sue her."

"I hope you're wrong," I said. Poor Grams. First her house caught fire and now she might be sued. It struck me that getting old can be an awful pain.

I went right home after school. I wanted to find out what had happened when she visited Mr. Wagner.

Grams was there with the twins.

"Did you go to the hospital?" I asked. She looked okay. In fact, she looked very good, almost excited. "How was Mr. Wagner?"

"Actually, he's doing very well," Grams said.

"Was he mad?"

"No, he's really a charming man and very understanding. Particularly when I told him how upset I was and how I thought I shouldn't drive anymore. He said, nonsense, that everybody has accidents, it has nothing to do with age. He's sorry he let his daughter sell his car. But when he lived alone, she was always phoning and coming over to check up when she knew he had the car out. That's why he lives at Cherry Garden. She wanted him to live with her, but he said he would go crazy."

"I guess you're glad," I said. "I mean, he's not going to sue you or anything."

"No," Grams said. "He admitted that he should have been paying more attention when he crossed the street, and the best part is, I didn't run over him twice after all."

"How's that?" I asked.

"When I went forward the second time, he was trying to get up and the bumper just pushed him down again."

"Good," I said.

Grams was still talking about Mr. Wagner at dinner.

"You and Mr. Wagner seem to have gotten along very well," Ma said.

"It was just amazing. We have so much in common. He used to have an antique store, and he and his late wife, Madeline, would go over to Europe on buying trips, just the way Chris's father and I would when we restocked the gallery. Why, we could have been over there at the same time."

"Are you going to visit him again?" Dennie asked.

"I wouldn't advise that," Pop said.

"For heaven's sake, why not?" Grams looked at Pop.

"You don't know anything about this Mr. Wagner," Pop said. "For all you know, he could be sweet-talking you. He could even be planning to sue you."

"Sweet-talking! Honestly, Christopher. I'm not a child. I think I'm perfectly capable of deciding how sincere a person is." Grams's expression reminded me of the twins' when they're being stubborn.

"Even so," Pop said. "He's a stranger to us."

"I told him I'd drive him to Cherry Garden from the hospital tomorrow, and regardless of what you say, I'm going to. It's the least I can do. But don't worry, Elizabeth, I'll pick up the twins on my way home." Grams laid down her fork. "It's been a very busy day. I think I'll turn in."

Before Pop could say anything, Grams had left the kitchen. Pop turned to Ma. "What's gotten into her?"

"If you ask me, she sounds like she's got a thing for this Mr. Wagner. I think it's cute," Dennie said, looking at the clock. "I have to go. The store is having a midnight madness sale."

"What time are you through?" Pop asked.

"Don't worry," Dennie said. "Bruce is driving me home."

For the next couple of weeks, Grams didn't mention Mr. Wagner. I guessed she decided Pop was right and he couldn't be trusted. That's why I was shocked when Grams suddenly said at breakfast on Saturday, "I won't be home for dinner tonight. Harold and I are going to the opera."

"Harold?" Pop asked. "Harold who?"

"Harold Wagner, of course," Grams said. "The doctor has given him a walking cast, so we thought we'd celebrate by going to the opera. Can you imagine, that Cherry Garden makes him sign out as if he were a child. They even wanted to know what time he would be back!"

Pop frowned. "I didn't know you'd seen that man again. How many times have you talked with him?"

"I'm not a child," Grams said. "I don't have to have my friends or where or when I go approved by you."

The rest of us stared first at Grams and then at Pop.

Pop sputtered for a minute and then he said, "I wasn't saying you should."

"I should hope not," Grams said.

Later that day I went into the living room to watch the sports results on TV. Dennie had the news on.

"Isn't it cute that Grams is dating Mr. Wagner?" Dennie asked me.

"How did you know Grams was dating Mr. Wagner?" I sat down beside her on the couch.

"Of course, you wouldn't know Grams was seeing Mr. Wagner. All you do is hang out in your room and the kitchen."

"That's not true," I said.

"Sure! When was the last time you sat in the living room with the rest of the family?"

"I'm in the living room now. It's not my fault nobody's here. Besides, I don't see you hanging around much."

"I'm not the one who doesn't know what's going on," Dennie said.

"Pop didn't know either," I said.

"Men," Dennie said.

"It really seems weird to me: old people dating. I mean, do you think they kiss and stuff?"

"Honestly, if they feel like kissing, why shouldn't they? In our death and dying class we learned that senior citizens are often sexually active."

I stared at her.

"You know, Andy, it's time you grew up," Dennie said. "You act as if everything is some kind of joke or as if it doesn't concern you at all. Look at that poor girl who asked you to her party. I bet you didn't even give her a civil answer. And you treat Molly as if she's less than human. It'll serve you right if she starts dating one of your stupid friends."

For a moment I was speechless. "Which of my friends is Molly after?" I finally asked.

"I don't know," Dennie said. "I just said it was possible. And why does she have to be the one who's after someone? Maybe one of your friends is after her."

The sports section of the news came on. I watched it, then went into the kitchen. Ma was standing at the kitchen table surrounded by a million pans and bowls.

"What are you doing?" I asked.

"Baking Christmas cookies." Ma moved a bowl to one side and picked up a spoon.

"How come? Not that I'm complaining, you understand."

"Oh, it just seemed a Christmassy thing to do."

I was surprised. It had been years since Ma had baked Christmas cookies.

"Where's Grams?" I asked.

"She's in her room. She's going to get her hair done later. Why? Don't you think I'm capable of baking cookies without her supervision?"

"Gee, Ma, kind of touchy, aren't you?"

"That's putting it mildly." Ma banged a cookie sheet down on the counter. "How much longer do you think it'll be until her house is finished?"

"Pop said the kitchen was going pretty slowly."

Ma dropped little mounds of dough on the cookie sheet and then shoved it into the oven. "Frankly, I don't think she's in any great hurry." She wiped her hands on a paper towel and started to grease another tray.

I dipped my finger into the bowl of cookie dough. As far as I'm concerned, baking cookies is a waste of energy. Nothing tastes better than uncooked dough. "You think she likes living like this?" I asked.

"Don't you start in on the size of this house," Ma said. "We were getting along perfectly fine until Grams moved in."

That wasn't strictly true. Sleeping in a closet-size room with a dog wasn't my idea of getting along fine.

"I think she likes being in the middle of things and having people to boss," Ma continued. "I had hoped she'd miss her art gallery, but she doesn't seem terribly concerned about it."

"Well, it's great she's home for the twins," I said. "It certainly makes things a lot less complicated."

Ma gave me a dirty look. "For you maybe," she said, then added, "but it's an ill wind."

"What do you mean?"

"I don't like feeling like a guest in my own house."

"Maybe she and Mr. Wagner will get married and move into her house." I threw that out to see what Ma's reaction would be.

"Andy! What are you saying? Do you know something?"

"How would I know anything?" I said. "Would you like Grams to get married again?"

"I can't say it would bother me," Ma said. "But I think your father would be pretty upset."

"Why?"

Before Ma could answer, we heard the sound of Grams's heels coming down the hall. Grams wears high heels all the time, even if she isn't going anywhere.

"Smells good," Grams said as she came into the kitchen. "Are you making those butterscotch icebox cookies that Christopher loves? Andy." She suddenly noticed what I was doing. "Stop eating that raw dough, it will give you worms."

"How ridiculous," Ma said. "That's just an old wives' tale. There is absolutely nothing in the dough that could produce worms."

"I think you'll find science has discovered that plenty of old wives' tales, as people choose to call them, have more than a grain of truth in them," Grams said. "And the medical community no longer encourages ingesting raw eggs."

"Why not?" I asked.

"Uncooked eggs can have the salmonella germ in them, and the eggs in that dough are uncooked."

I made a face and went over and dropped the lump of dough into the garbage can.

"Good boy," Grams said.

Ma ignored us. She was busy pulling a sheet of cookies out of the oven. Grams leaned over to look at them.

"Oatmeal," she declared. "Christopher never liked oatmeal."

"He does now," Ma said. "And the kids love them."

"Well, I suppose you know what you're doing. I'm going to get my hair done, and I have to pick up my good dress at the cleaner's. I hope they got the smell of smoke out of it. Now, where did I put my purse?"

I picked it up from a chair and handed it to her.

She was almost out of the kitchen when she turned around. "Oh, I almost forgot. I won't be home for Christmas dinner: I'm having it at Harold's daughter's house. But we'll be here for dessert. I thought that would work out better, since we can have dessert and coffee in the living room, which would be much more pleasant than eating in the kitchen."

A few minutes after Grams left, Pop came in. "Cookies! What a great idea. It really seems like Christmas now."

When Ma told Pop that Grams wasn't going to spend Christmas Day with us, he acted as if it was Ma's fault. "What an insane thing to say," he said to her.

"Don't get mad at me," Ma said. "It wasn't my idea."

Then he began to act as if Ma had misunderstood.

"You can't mean she's spending the holiday with a total stranger?" he asked.

When Ma nodded her head, he said, "Why? Did she explain why?"

"No. Why don't you ask her?"

"She prefers the company of strangers over her own grandchildren?" Pop said, more to himself than to Ma and me. Then he asked, "Has she been seeing this man often? I'm sure she doesn't realize how it looks, spending the holiday with him. Why, he might think they're serious or something. And she's never brought him home. Can you tell me why that is? Doesn't she want us to meet him? Why is she hiding him?"

Ma calmly dumped the dirty bowl and cookie sheets into

the sink. "I wouldn't say she's hiding him exactly," she said. "Don't forget his foot has been in a cast and he's needed crutches. I'm sure up until now stairs have been very difficult for him to manage."

Pop grunted.

"Then again," Ma continued, "maybe she's afraid of how you'd act."

"And what is that supposed to mean?" Pop picked up one of the cookies off the rack and bit into it.

"You're not very nice to Dennie's boyfriends," I suggested.

"My God, are you saying he acts like Bruce?" Pop asked. "Where did you meet him?"

"I've never met him," I said. "I didn't mean anything." I decided not to tell Pop what Martin had said about Mr. Wagner.

11

POP IS USUALLY INTO CHRISTMAS. HE MAKES PICK-
ing out a tree this huge family project. I remember when I was
a kid sloshing around damp lots while Pop examined one tree
after another. It was really boring. He didn't want us to bring
friends and he wouldn't let us run around.

But when he heard that Grams wouldn't be with us for
dinner, he started to lose interest. Then Grandma and Grandpa
Reid wrote to say that a friend invited them to go with her on
a Christmas cruise to Mexico.

"Grandma and Grandpa won't be here?" Molly asked. "But
they're always here."

"Their trip sounds like fun," Dennie said.

"They're doing it for a friend who was recently widowed,"
Ma explained. "She and her husband had planned this trip, and
somehow she had gotten the idea her late husband would still
want her to go."

"Sounds like a sick idea to me," Pop said. "What's the matter with everybody? Christmas isn't the time to go running off to a foreign country."

Usually our tree is up and decorated two weeks before Christmas, but here it was, a few days before, and our living room was bare. Finally Dennie said, "You know, Dad, most of the tree lots have been picked clean. Bruce and I were driving home from the movies last night and one lot was almost sold out. They were selling any tree in the place for twenty dollars."

Ma looked at Pop, and when he didn't reply, she said to Dennie, "Why don't you and Bruce buy one of them if they're not too straggly."

"Can we go with you?" the twins asked.

"Sure," Dennie said. "Bruce and I are going to a party tonight, but we'll pick up a tree first and then bring you guys home."

It was hard to believe that Pop was going to let Bruce buy our Christmas tree. And his attitude about Christmas became contagious, because two days before, Ma said, "Why should I fuss with a turkey? It's such a mess, and most of you don't even like it. I think I'll have a nice ham."

"Why not," Pop said. Then he added, "I can't understand why Grams would go over to a stranger's house on Christmas. And with that terrible man."

"Now, Chris," Ma said. "You haven't even met Mr. Wagner. How can you say he's terrible?"

Pop didn't answer. He only sighed and wandered out of the kitchen.

The twins were the only ones who were excited. They still believed in Santa Claus, so on Christmas morning they were running around and screaming about all the stuff under the tree. Grams gave the twins their own two-wheel bikes. They almost went out of their minds when they saw them. So did Ma.

"The bikes are much too big," she said. "They couldn't possibly manage them."

"Nonsense," Grams said. "They come with training wheels. It's silly to buy a bike too small. This way they can grow into them."

"It's very dangerous to let children grow into bikes. They need bikes they can handle," Ma argued.

"Put on the extra wheels," the twins begged. "We want to ride them."

"Later," Ma said. "Open the rest of your gifts, and then we have to get ready for church. Besides, it's raining outside. Put the bikes in the garage until I see if they're the right size. Andy, help them."

"Come on, guys." I put down the electric razor Grams had given me. I don't shave yet, but I looked on it as a vote of confidence that someday I would.

Grams gave Ma a microwave oven. When I saw it, I wondered if Ma would be offended. She had said she wanted one, but since this one had come from Grams, she might think Grams was criticizing her cooking. Fortunately, Ma seemed to consider it a sign that Grams wasn't going to be in her kitchen forever. Pop got a new recliner. Grams had had it delivered when Pop was at work, and kept it in her room.

"You always look so tired, Christopher." Grams patted his arm. "You really work much too hard."

Grams gave Molly and Dennie each a little box. They held pieces of family jewelry. Dennie went crazy over her ring.

"It belonged to my grandmother," Grams explained. "It's always gone to the oldest girl in the family."

Dennie squealed and hugged Grams and put it on immediately. Molly got a pin. She didn't say much about it. I know she rarely wears jewelry, and I never see many girls wearing pins in high school.

After we got back from church, Grams went off to her room and Pop went down to the garage to attach the training wheels to the twins' bikes. I guess Ma had agreed to let them keep them. Dennie borrowed Grams's car for a few hours so she could visit Bruce, and Molly phoned Jennie. After she had been on the phone for a few minutes, she hung up and yelled, "I'm going over to Jennie's and then to Cherry Garden. I'm supposed to help at that Christmas lunch." She poked her head into the living room. "Want to come?" she asked. "Martin said he thought he'd go, too, since he knows some of the people there from last year."

"I can think of better things to do with my Christmas than serve a bunch of old people," I said, clicking the remote control on the TV.

"Suit yourself." Molly grabbed her jacket off the chair where she'd dumped it after church and left.

The house was incredibly quiet. I sat alone in the living room, watching an ancient black-and-white movie.

"Andy," Ma said when she saw me sitting there, "if you're lonely, you can come and help me peel the potatoes."

"That's okay," I said. "I'm going to take Daisy for a walk."

"It's raining," Ma said.

"Hey, she still has to go out." I got off the couch and went to look for the dog's leash. "Where is Daisy, anyway?"

"Down in the garage."

I called for Daisy. Since she heard me shaking her leash, she came bounding up the stairs. Once I was outside, I found it wasn't raining very hard. I had nowhere in particular to go, so we went over to Golden Gate Park. I pretty much had the park to myself except that I kept passing groups of homeless people who were camping in the sheltered groves of trees and bushes. They looked pretty miserable, huddled in plastic bags and covered with wet newspapers. They stared at us as we passed, and I tried not to look at them. I wished I had brought some money.

This Christmas was turning out to be a real bummer. By the time I got home, Dennie was back and Grams had left for Cherry Garden. She and Harold were going to his daughter's from there.

The twins came up from the garage complaining, "Why did it have to rain on Christmas? When will it stop?"

"Stop whining," Pop snapped. He picked up the newspaper and sat down on the couch. I wondered why he didn't sit in his new recliner. "Look at this." He slapped his hand across a sheet of the paper. "Ads and sales. Where are people supposed to get money to buy stuff after Christmas?"

"They take gifts back and exchange them," Dennie said. "Don't you know, the day after Christmas is one of the biggest shopping days of the year?"

"I thought this was a religious holiday," Pop said.

Ma came out of the kitchen and looked at us. "Honestly, what is the matter with all of you?"

"It doesn't seem like Christmas," Anne said.

Alice nodded her head. "Grandma and Grandpa and Grams aren't here."

"It's a terrible thing," Pop said, "when a grandmother would rather spend Christmas with total strangers than with her grandchildren."

Ma burst out laughing. "That is the silliest thing I ever

92

heard. My parents aren't here either, and I'm not making such a fuss."

Pop growled under his breath.

We had dinner earlier than usual because Ma wanted to clean up the kitchen before Grams and Harold arrived for dessert. Ma set out fancy coffee cups and plates. She made a pot of coffee and put on some water to boil in case Harold preferred tea. Then we waited.

I got so bored I played one of the twins' stupid new board games with them. Molly was back on the phone with Jennie, and Bruce came over. He and Dennie went into the kitchen to get a soft drink. I thought they were gone an awfully long time. Usually when they do things like that, Pop gets antsy and starts making excuses to spy on them, but he was so busy grumbling about why Grams didn't come home I don't think he noticed.

It was almost eight, and Pop had gone from being angry to being worried, when the front door banged open and Grams marched in and started down the hall to her room.

"Grams?" Ma called. "Isn't Harold with you?"

Grams came into the living room. "He's not coming," she said. "I hope that won't inconvenience you."

"But what happened?" Ma asked.

"If you don't mind, I think I'll go to bed." With that remark, Grams left. Then I heard her door slam.

For a minute we all sat there and then Pop stood up. "Why are we sitting here? I don't know about the rest of you, but I'm starving. How about some of that pumpkin pie?" For the first time that day, Pop actually looked happy.

"Since we're not having company," Ma said, "let's go back to the kitchen. There's no point in getting spots on the rug."

We all stood up. The day had been so incredibly boring—even Bruce was unusually quiet—that any activity seemed like a good idea. Without saying anything, we filed into the kitchen.

Ma set the table with our kitchen plates and cut the pies. She looked over at the twins. "It's been a very long day. You two, eat your pie and then start to get ready for bed. You've been up since five."

It was quiet at the table. When the phone rang, we all jumped.

"Who could be phoning at this hour?" Ma asked.

"It's only eight-thirty," Dennie said.

"I've got it," Grams called from the hall.

Pop stopped looking so happy.

Grams came into the kitchen. She had her coat over her arm. "That was Harold," she said. "I'm going over to Cherry Garden for a little while. I shouldn't be too late."

"Mother, it's dark. You can't go driving around alone at night. Whatever you have to say to this Harold person can wait until morning."

"Hey, Mrs. H.," Bruce said, "Dennie and I will drive you." He looked over to Dennie for approval. She nodded her head.

Leave it to Bruce to figure out a legitimate way to leave this funeral.

"That's very sweet of you two, and I'll take you up on it," Grams said. She smiled at Pop. "I won't be too late."

Before Pop could protest again, Grams, Dennie, and Bruce left.

"Molly, Andy, clear up these dishes, please. I'm putting Alice and Anne to bed." Ma became very busy. "Come on, girls, you've played enough with that pie. Maybe it will stop raining tomorrow and you can ride your bikes."

Molly and I picked up the plates. Pop was still sitting at the table. He was chasing a crumb of crust around the dish with his fork.

Molly loaded the dishes in the dishwasher. I was supposed to put the food away.

"Want more pie?" I asked Pop.

Pop looked at his plate as if he was surprised it was empty. "I can't imagine what your grandmother is thinking of," he said.

I took that to mean a no to another piece of pie, so I covered it and put it in the refrigerator with the rest of the food. Then I figured I'd had enough family, so I gathered my gifts from under the tree and went into my room.

My gifts didn't make much of a pile. I bet the twins' stuff practically covered their floor. The older you get, the smaller the pile of gifts, I decided. There was nothing wrong with my stuff, it's just that it wasn't all that exciting—clothes, books, a new wallet, and, of course, the shaver. I took it out of the box and examined it. I hoped it would still work when I was ready to use it. I dropped it into a drawer. I wished someone had given me my own TV. It would have been nice to crawl into bed and have something to watch. I turned on my CD, making sure it wasn't too loud. Pop was ready to explode, and I didn't want to be the one to light the fuse.

I was almost asleep when I heard Daisy pawing at my door. I opened it, and she made a flying leap onto my bed. I heard Grams and Dennie come into the kitchen. They were giggling.

"It was silly of me to get angry," I heard Grams say. "After all, it wasn't Harold's fault his daughter was acting so terribly. Honestly, she made me feel as if I were some kind of gold digger. I felt positively immoral."

"I wouldn't worry about his daughter," Dennie said. "And thanks again for the ring. I love it."

"I'm glad, dear. I looked at all that jewelry and I realized that it could have been burned up in the fire and then I thought, this is so silly. Why should Dennie and Molly have to wait until I'm dead to get it. They should be able to enjoy it now, while they're young."

They must have moved toward the hall, because I couldn't hear them anymore. I nudged Daisy off my leg. I couldn't imagine why Harold's daughter was so nasty to Grams any more than I could understand why Pop seemed to dislike Mr. Wagner. It's none of your business, I told myself. In a way, I wished vacation was over. Life was a lot less complicated when I was in school.

OUR SEMESTER DIDN'T END AT THE START OF THE Christmas holidays. No, that would be too humane. The teachers let all the papers and final exams hang over our heads, making sure we couldn't enjoy our freedom.

Of course, Molly spent the week between Christmas and New Year's Day working on her Bay Area social concerns paper. She was always going over to Cherry Garden. Grams was at Cherry Garden a lot, too, which meant I had to watch the twins because the store where Dennie worked had its big after-Christmas sale and she was there every day.

Five movies for little kids were showing, but Ma wouldn't agree to the twins spending every afternoon in "some dark theater when they could be out in the fresh air."

That seemed a strange thing to say, since it had been raining almost every day since Christmas and the twins just sat in the house watching TV.

I did take them to two movies. It was kind of fun because they got so excited. I mean, they really believed what they were seeing on the screen. They laughed out loud at the funny scenes and Alice covered her eyes at the scary parts. Seeing them so much for that week made me realize how different they both are. It seemed as if the whole family always referred to them in plural: "The twins did this, the twins did that." But as I watched them trying to learn to ride their bikes in the garage, it was obvious that Anne was the bossy, domineering one and that Alice pretty much followed her lead.

Coming out of the second movie, we ran into three of their friends.

"This is our big brother." Anne pulled at my arm to make me stop.

"Yes," Alice chimed in. "He's teaching us to ride our new bikes."

"And he plays games with us," Anne finished.

They sounded like Ma when she's bragging about one of us. I felt silly. The three friends and one of their mothers looked at me and I looked at them.

"You must be a big help at home," the mother finally said. I just nodded.

One kid pulled at my jacket. "Hi," he said.

"Hi, yourself," I said. "Come on." I motioned to the twins. "We have to get going."

"See you at school," Anne yelled at them as I dragged her away.

"We told you he was big," Alice said to one of her friends before I grabbed her.

When we got home, I took them outside and ran up and down the street holding on to their bikes so they could keep their balance. I felt I had to do something to live up to their view of me.

On New Year's Eve, Dennie and Bruce went to a party. Grams suggested to Ma that it would be nice if she and Harold double-dated with Ma and Pop.

"Why would I want to do that?" Pop asked.

"Because he's a friend of your mother's," Ma said. "And you kept saying how he is a stranger. Well, now he won't be a stranger."

"I hope this doesn't encourage her," Pop said. "She might think I approve of her gallivanting around. Whatever happened to the sweet little grandmother she used to be?"

"Your mother was never a sweet little grandmother and you know it," Ma said. "And I don't think it matters if you approve or not. You're not her father."

"I'm beginning to think I should be her guardian," Pop complained. But he finally agreed to the arrangement.

Since neither Molly nor I had any plans, we were stuck baby-sitting the twins. We told them they could stay up to midnight, but they fell asleep on the couch around ten-thirty. Molly made popcorn and the two of us sat watching celebrations roll across the country on the TV screen.

"I'm so sick of waiting to really live," Molly said.

I looked at her. "That's a stupid thing to say. What are we doing now?"

"Waiting," Molly said.

"Waiting for what?"

"Oh, I don't know, to be able to drive, to date, to wear makeup. Look at us, sitting here like a couple of dweebs."

"Hey, speak for yourself." I got up and wandered over to the TV to look for the remote. I was sick of watching some manic bandleader trying to whip a crowd of people into a frenzy because the second hand had crept forward and a new year had begun.

"Don't you feel like you're not doing anything?" Molly continued.

"I do lots of things," I argued. "I play soccer." I stopped to think. "I hang out with my friends. I go to school . . ." My voice trailed off. I couldn't think of anything else I was doing except maybe taking Daisy for walks and watching the twins. "Well," I concluded, "next year I'll be getting my driver's license, and after that I'll be old enough to get a job."

"See," Molly said. "You are waiting. What kind of a girl would you like to go out with?"

"What makes you ask that?" I started to shout, but then I remembered the twins, so I lowered my voice. "Why would I want to go out with a girl? I'm surrounded by girls. Everywhere I turn in this house, there's another girl. Even Daisy's a girl." Daisy raised her head at the sound of her name and thumped the floor with her tail. "No offense." I reached over and patted her. "Why would I want to get involved with another girl?"

"You're as insensitive as Dennie keeps saying," Molly said. "Most of the guys in your class have girlfriends." She suddenly changed the subject, or I thought she changed the subject. "Does Martin have a girlfriend?"

"What do you care?" I asked. "You leave Martin alone," which was a stupid thing for me to say because Martin is certainly perfectly capable of taking care of himself. He has as many sisters as I do.

"What are you getting so excited about?" Molly said.

Fortunately, Alice fell off the couch and started to cry and then Anne woke up, so I didn't have to try and explain.

"Is it New Year's yet?" Anne said.

"You missed it," I answered. "Time to go to bed."

Ma and Pop never mentioned what happened New Year's Eve, and I never asked. I had a feeling it wasn't a roaring success because Grams was decidedly unfriendly to Pop the next day.

School started and I had to finish all the papers that I had put off working on. The real bummer was when the coach took me aside and told me I didn't make the team.

"Not make the team?" I said. "But I showed up for all the practices just like you asked."

"Showing up isn't enough, Halliday. You got to do more than just be there. Maybe next year. Meanwhile, bone up on developing some team spirit."

I really didn't know what he was talking about, but I felt too intimidated to ask him.

After final exams, we got one day at the end of January for a break and then the new semester started. None of my classes really changed except for religion. I finished modern social issues and signed up for something called alternatives to violence.

At dinner on the first day of the new semester, Pop started grilling us on our classes. Our report cards had just arrived in the mail, and he wasn't exactly pleased with my grades. I was passing. What more did he want?

"You're taking alternatives to violence?" Pop asked me. "What kind of class is that?"

"You won't like it," Dennie predicted.

"Why not?" I said. "I don't think I'm a violent person."

"Sure," Dennie said. "I still say you won't like it. It's a weird class. It's sort of a cross between a debating team and the martial arts. The best part is that Mr. Clark, the teacher, tries to have boy/girl pairs. He likes to see the different ways males and females solve problems. There's a lot of talk about society's rights and individual rights and civil disobedience. You know, do people have a right to protest, that kind of thing. You practically have to memorize the Declaration of Independence. Mr. Clark was always telling us how he abhors violence, but it seems to me he was always trying to provoke fights."

I swallowed hard.

"That sounds like a very strange class," Grams said. "High school has certainly changed since I was a girl. We were never encouraged to argue and insult people. I don't know what happened to plain old-fashioned reticence. Dennie, what are you taking?"

"Marriage and family life. All the seniors have to take it. This year they're letting us pick our mates instead of just assigning them. Luckily, Bruce and I are in the same class, so we'll get to be a couple and get married."

Pop started making choking noises. He gagged for a minute before he managed to take a deep breath. "What did you say?"

Dennie laughed. "Cool down, Dad. This class is supposed to make us think twice about getting married too young. Mr. Hales makes us pretend to marry somebody in the class, and then we have to figure out how we're going to manage. You know, how to try to go to college and work and buy food and rent an apartment and who should do the cooking and cleaning. By the end of the class we have to find a way to fit a baby into the budget. Mr. Hales runs the class like a board game. We pick cards each week. Some of the cards have things like the water heater bottom fell out and flooded the room and all your clothes were ruined, or the car was totaled and you have to find another way to get to work. Last year, one couple pulled a card that said they had triplets. I think those two decided to go home to their parents. But if you do that, your grade is lowered."

"Can I have more milk?" Anne asked.

"I'll get it." Pop got up. "I need a break from this conversation."

"Speaking of marriage," Grams said, "Harold and I have decided to do it."

It took me a second before what she had said sunk in. Pop was getting the carton of milk from the refrigerator. The carton slipped out of his fingers and crashed on the floor. It was full and split wide open. The milk didn't puddle on the floor, neat and tidy—no, it exploded. It sprayed up, dousing all of us. The twins started squealing.

"Well," Grams said with a little laugh. "I thought it was appropriate to throw rice at the happy couple, not milk."

I snickered.

Ma leaped up from the table. She gave Pop a nudge. He was still standing staring at Grams, not noticing the milk that was eddying all around him. Ma started pulling paper towels off the roll.

"Don't play with the milk," she said to Anne. "Help wipe it up."

Daisy, who had been dozing on the couch in the living room, came barreling in. She started running around Pop's feet, licking up the milk.

Ma pushed at Daisy with her foot. "Get that dog out of here. She just makes the floor even stickier."

No one had said anything to Grams. She sat there quietly, her hands folded in her lap.

Finally Dennie got up and hugged her. "I think it's great about you and Harold," she said. "You should come to our marriage and family class and give a talk about it never being too late or something like that. Actually, it would have been even better if you had come to my death and dying class."

Grams looked stunned. "Death and dying?" she repeated.

"Don't pay any attention to the name. It really should be called life and living, or maybe living and dying, if they want to get the dying part in. We ended with old people." Dennie stopped. "Older people," she amended. "We learned how older people are stereotyped and everything."

"Dennie," Ma said, "will you please stop pestering Grams and wipe up the milk you're tracking all over the floor, and don't call Mr. Wagner Harold. It's not respectful."

"I think he would like that," Grams said. "Yes, all of you can feel free to call him Harold."

"I can't believe you," Pop suddenly said.

We all turned to look at him. He was still in the same spot.

"Believe what?" Ma was still trying to get him to move so she could dry the floor.

He impatiently waved her off. "At your age, thinking of getting married again. And to someone you've only known for a few weeks."

"I know him," Molly said. "He doesn't like living at Cherry Garden."

"Martin told me how he tried to run away once while he was visiting his daughter," I remarked. "The hospital found him and made him go back."

"What kind of behavior is that for a grown man?" Pop asked. "Running away? He sounds like he might be senile."

"You can't fault him for wanting to be independent." Grams calmly picked up her coffee cup. "Really, Christopher, stop frowning at me. Harold is a perfectly respectable man, and at

104

our age, time is relative. He's a widower, and he has two children, a very bossy daughter and a son who's an engineer and lives in some jungle. He has two grandchildren, an adequate pension, and some stock, if money is what's bothering you. Not that it matters to me. Your father left me very comfortable, and there's the art gallery. Actually, it might be a lark if we decided to run it together. Harold doesn't know much about art, but he's very knowledgeable about antiques and running a business. And for your information, he is in perfect control of all his faculties."

"You would let this Harold manage my father's gallery?" Pop looked really wild. He had run his fingers through his hair and it was standing on end. I can't remember when I saw him look this mad, not even the time when I was mucking around with a chemistry set and made a stink bomb that smelled so bad a neighbor called the police.

"Now, that's just enough, Christopher," Grams said sharply. "It was not your father's business, it was our business, your father and me." She stopped. "That doesn't sound very grammatical, does it? Well, never mind, you know what I mean. You never had any interest in art or running the gallery, which was fine. But don't act as if Harold were stealing something from you."

Grams folded her napkin, although why she bothered, I don't know—it was just a paper one—and got up.

"I invited Harold over for dinner this Saturday night. I assumed he would be welcome?"

"Of course he's welcome," Ma said. "We'd be delighted to have him over." She glanced at Pop to see if he would agree with her. Pop didn't say anything. "And I think Harold is very nice."

"Thank you, Elizabeth, I appreciate that." Grams picked up her dishes and put them in the sink. "And now if you'll excuse me."

Molly said, "I think Harold is the neatest old man I ever met."

Grams gave Molly a hug. "That's a sweet thing to say. And you, Andy, what do you think about this?"

"Yeah," I said. "Well, whatever's right."

"I'll take that as an approval."

When she left the kitchen, Pop asked, "What could she be thinking of? I can't believe that she actually plans to marry that man."

"Will you stop referring to him as 'that man'?" Ma said.

"Is he going to be your stepfather?" Molly asked. "Will that make him our step-grandfather?"

"What do you mean by that?" Pop frowned at her.

"Nothing," Molly said.

"Getting married at her age: it's indecent," Pop said.

"Actually, that's not true," Dennie said. "In our death and dying class—"

"Forget that class!" Pop yelled. "Any school that would encourage you to marry a cretin like Bruce lacks a certain credibility in my book. Thinking of Bruce being the father of my grandchildren makes me wonder if it was all worth it."

Dennie's face got purple at Pop's remark about Bruce, but before she could say anything, Ma quickly interrupted. "I think we've all said enough for one night. Dennie, you and Molly give the twins their baths, please. Andy, clean up the kitchen and wash the floor; it's still sticky. The mop is in the broom closet."

I started to protest—I mean, why should I get the worst job—but Ma wasn't even looking at me. Instead, she was trying to get Pop out of the kitchen. "Come on, dear, we can talk in the bedroom."

I started to pick up the plates. In spite of Ma's efforts, Pop was still standing in the middle of the kitchen. "Maybe she did more than sprain her wrist. Maybe she hit her head when she fell," he said.

"This is ridiculous." Ma began to sound angry. "Your mother is a grown woman who has a right to her own life. Now, will you get out of the way so Andy can do his job?"

13

THE ATMOSPHERE IN OUR HOUSE FOR THE REST OF the week was strange, as if we were all waiting for an explosion. We talked in whispers, and whenever Pop came into a room, the rest of us would stop talking. We all felt guilty even though we hadn't done anything.

Grams spent a lot of time discussing the dinner with Dennie, Molly, and Ma. "The kitchen table will be so crowded," she said once.

"Maybe we could send the twins over to Susie's that night," Ma suggested. She sounded sincere and not sarcastic, the way she often did when she talked to Grams. Ever since Grams had announced that she was going to get married, Ma had become incredibly friendly.

"And have them eaten alive by that terrible child? After all, she bit Alice once," Grams said. "Besides, I don't want to make a big deal of this; that would make Harold uncomfortable. I want a pleasant family dinner. I only hope Chris behaves himself. Speak to him, Elizabeth. Maybe he'll listen to you."

I couldn't believe that Grams was admitting to Ma that Ma understood Pop better than she did.

"I doubt if it would help, but I'll try," Ma promised.

On Saturday, Grams and Ma were already in the kitchen when I got up.

"Good morning, Andy," Grams said. She turned back to Ma. "You know, the main problem with eating in the kitchen is having all the mess from cooking staring you in the face."

Ma nodded.

I opened the refrigerator. "Where's the milk?" I asked.

"Andy, get out of there," Ma said. "And don't touch anything."

"But I'm hungry," I said. I looked more closely. "What is that red stuff?"

"It's aspic," Grams said. "Here, move over, dear. I'll find the milk for you."

"I've been thinking," Ma said. "If we had more card tables, we could eat in the living room. It would be crowded, but that might make it seem cozy. What do you think?"

"It might work," Grams agreed.

"Andy, when you're finished slopping milk over the floor, would you run over to Martin's house and ask to borrow a couple of card tables? And see if your father will go with you to help carry them." She turned to Grams. "At least that will get Chris out of the house for a while."

"I should have anticipated this," Grams said. "Even when he was a little boy he would get upset when we had company. He would say, 'Why are these strange people here? Make them go home.' I'd hoped he'd outgrown that."

I carried my glass of milk and a handful of potato chips into the living room. Pop was slumped on the couch in front of the TV watching cartoons with a twin on either side of him. When I asked him whether he wanted to help me pick up card tables at Martin's, he just grunted.

"I'll go." Molly sat up from the recliner. "Wait a minute."

"That's okay, I can manage," I said.

"No, no, I want to talk to Jennie. Wait, please."

"Make it fast," I said.

I thought she'd be out in a few minutes; how long can it take to throw on jeans and a sweatshirt? But I watched several cartoons and she hadn't come back.

"Are you coming or not?" I yelled. "I haven't got all day."

"I'm ready, I'm ready, just a sec."

Five more minutes elapsed before she appeared. It was obvious what had taken her so long. She must have used Dennie's electric hair thing, because her usual straight hair was shaped into odd corkscrews. She had on eye makeup and some of it had flaked on her glasses. Her lipstick made her mouth look sort of lopsided. She was wearing jeans, but she had on one of Dennie's shiny blouses and was carrying her new jacket.

"What have you done?" I asked.

Pop turned away from the TV screen. "You look terrible," he said. "Wash that junk off."

"We haven't got time." I grabbed her arm. "She can do it when we get back." I shoved her out of the living room and down the hall to the front door.

"Thanks, Andy, that was nice of you."

"What do you mean, nice? I don't care if you look like a clown, but I have no intention of spending the whole day collecting a few card tables."

110

Martin answered the door. He was wearing his gym shorts and an old T-shirt that had a large hole in the middle. He looked half-asleep. "Kinda early, isn't it?" he asked. "Was I supposed to go somewhere with you?"

"I just came over to borrow some card tables from your mother," I said. "Molly's here to see Jennie."

Molly had been standing behind me, and when Martin noticed her, he retreated behind the door. Molly giggled.

"Jennie's not here," Martin said. "I'll ask my mother about the tables." He'd started to back down the hall when he stopped and said, "You can come in." He disappeared.

"Thanks," I said sarcastically. You'd think it was the first time either Molly or I had been in his house.

Martin's mother came out of the kitchen. Martin wasn't with her. "Hello, Andy. Molly, how grownup you look," she said. "Your mom phoned. I have the card tables in the kitchen. Where did Martin go? He can help you carry them. Isn't this exciting about your grandmother? Come on, I'll get you the tables."

I followed her to the kitchen. When I returned, Martin had reappeared. He was wearing jeans and a clean white T-shirt. He and Molly were talking.

I shoved a card table at Molly.

"Here," I said. "Let's get going."

"Martin!" His mother had followed me from the kitchen. "Don't let poor little Molly carry that heavy thing. Help her."

He jumped forward and grabbed the card table from Molly.

"That's not necessary," I explained. "Molly's as strong as an ox."

Mrs. Brown burst out laughing. "What a terrible thing to say about your sister."

I trailed along behind Martin and Molly, who carried a card table between them. Martin left us at our front door. It was just as well he hadn't come in because Grandma and Grandpa Reid had just shown up on one of their surprise visits. They were on their way to Arizona, but they wanted to share all their videos of the Christmas cruise. It was obvious no one had time to sit down and watch them, but Grandma and Grandpa are flexible.

"My, my, my," Grandma Reid kept saying when Grams told her the big news.

"Now, that's fine," Grandpa said and leaned over and gave Grams a big kiss. "Nobody should have to live alone," he declared and he gave Grandma a pinch. "Right, Ethel?"

"Bill!" Grandma giggled.

Ma looked surprised.

Grandpa winked at Grandma. "Where are you two love-birds going on your honeymoon?" he asked Grams. "You should go on a cruise. There's nothing like a cruise for a little romance, right?"

Grandma patted Grandpa's cheek. "Now, what can we do to help? By the way, where's Christopher?"

We could hear banging and crashing sounds coming from the basement.

"Is that Pop?" I asked.

Ma nodded.

"What's he doing?" I said. "It sounds as if he's moving furniture."

Ma sighed. "Andy, go down and tell him to come up and say hello to Grandma and Grandpa."

I had no idea why he would be moving stuff around in the

112

garage. I went downstairs. "Hey, Pop?" I called. "What's going on?"

Pop was over in the corner near the stairs. He turned around. "I was just seeing if I could find some room," he said.

He had moved the table so it was kitty-corner to the wall and now he was trying to push the buffet next to it.

"That looks like the sort of thing Martin and I used to do when we were making clubhouses," I said. I thought Pop would deny doing anything so silly, but he didn't. He wasn't laughing, either.

"Do you ever feel the walls are closing in around you?" he asked.

"I guess," I said.

"I do not understand people's mania for change," he said. "Why do you think that is?"

It didn't sound like a question that deserved an answer, so I didn't say anything for a few minutes, but he kept looking at me, so I said, "I don't know."

He nodded. "Nobody does. Take your grandmother. Why is she suddenly deciding to marry? I do not understand women." Pop pulled up a dining room chair and sat down. "Why would Grams want to get involved with a person like that Harold? She had a husband, a nice house, a good business, friends, a loving family."

I leaned against the buffet. "Well, Grandfather has been dead for a long time. I don't even remember him," I said. "And she likes Harold."

Pop looked at me. "And forty years of marriage are worth nothing? I guess you think if I died tomorrow, it would be all right for your mother to run off and marry the first man she sees?"

I was shocked. "I didn't say that exactly." I tried to imagine Ma with somebody else and couldn't. I mean, Ma and Pop just go together. Maybe that's why Pop was so upset. When he sees Grams he sees Grandfather, and if Grams gets married again it would be like Grandfather was forgotten. I wondered if Pop would get mad if I went back upstairs. This was a very weird conversation, and I wasn't sure what Pop wanted me to say.

"Ma sent me down to tell you Grandma and Grandpa Reid are here."

"I know that," Pop said. "You can hear that man from a mile away. Sit down." He indicated a dining room chair.

"Shouldn't we be helping Ma?"

"Why?"

I pulled the chair over.

"They all seem pretty excited about the dinner and everything," I explained.

"I'm sure they can manage." Pop stretched out and tilted the chair so that it was resting on its two back legs. This drives Ma crazy.

As if on cue, Ma opened the door of my room. "What are you two doing down there?"

I waited for Pop to answer. When he didn't, I called up, "Nothing."

"Well, stop doing nothing. Chris, come up here and see my parents. Andy, how about taking the twins to the movies to get them out of my hair?"

"What about Molly?" I called.

"Molly's polishing the silver."

I considered arguing, but decided taking the twins to the movies was better than coping with Pop's strange mood.

"Okay," I said. "Sorry, Pop."

He nodded.

I thought he would follow me up the stairs, but he didn't. He just sat on the chair, half-hidden by the buffet.

By the time the twins and I got home from the movies, Grams had returned with Harold. Ma grabbed the twins at the door. "Quick, change your clothes," she said to me. "You and Molly can help serve the food."

Actually, Harold was very friendly. I don't know why Martin had found him so crabby. Harold asked Dennie what she planned to do in the future and if she had thought about a career in retailing. He talked to Molly about chess and to me about soccer. He and Grandpa talked trucks. Ma, Grams, Grandma, and Dennie talked about wedding plans. Between eating and answering questions, Molly and I brought dishes from the kitchen that looked better than they tasted. Then we took other dishes away. Pop did nothing. He didn't talk, he hardly ate, he didn't even flinch when Anne spilled her milk.

Dinner was almost over when Grandpa got up from the card table he was sharing with Grams and Harold. "Now everybody don't move. Ethel and I have a little surprise." He tapped me on the shoulder. "Come on, Andy. You can help us." Grandma and Grandpa were giggling like crazy. "I drove all over town trying to find this," Grandpa said when we got to the kitchen.

I didn't have a clue what "this" was.

"Run down and get the cake box that's in the dryer."

"The dryer?" I repeated.

"Had to hide it somewhere," Grandpa said.

I shook my head. Suddenly it seemed as if all the adults I knew were acting like a bunch of lunatics.

"Don't forget the champagne that's in the washing machine," Grandma said. She was lining up a set of wineglasses on the kitchen counter.

"And don't let Daisy up," she called after me.

Daisy was very happy to see me. She raced up and down the stairs a couple of times before collapsing in front of me.

"Sorry, old girl," I said. "You'll have to stay down here. You'll spoil the party."

I pulled a pink bakery box from the dryer and opened the lid of the washer. There were two bottles of champagne and one of sparkling apple juice leaning against the agitator. I decided I'd better make two trips.

"Just look," Grandma said when I placed the box on the table. "Your grandpa had a terrible time finding one." She opened the box and pulled out what looked like a miniature wedding cake, complete with a couple on the top.

I brought up the bottles and Grandma arranged the glasses on a tray. She put the cake on Ma's fancy platter. "Now, Andy, open the door."

"Surprise, surprise," Grandpa shouted. "An engagement deserves a celebration."

When everyone had a glass in front of them, filled with either champagne or apple juice, Grandpa stood up.

"A toast," he said. "To the happy couple. May you have as much joy with each other as Ethel and I have had."

"Why, Bill," Grandma said, "that was just beautiful."

Grandpa blushed and sat down. I noticed he had apple juice in his glass.

"Thank you," Grams said. Harold nodded and looked pleased. Then we all looked at Pop.

"Chris?" Ma said. "I think it's your turn."

Pop didn't stand up and give a toast. He stood up and

spilled his glass of wine all over himself. He reached for a napkin and started to mop his pants.

"I'll have to change," he said.

Ma looked stunned. The rest of us stared at the cake on our plates. Ten minutes passed and Pop still didn't come back.

Finally Grandpa leaned over and took Grams's hand. "I thought a special evening like this deserves a night on the town. What do you say?"

Grams looked around at the living room filled with card tables, dirty dishes, and people.

Dennie jumped to her feet. "I think that's a great idea," she said. "Molly, Andy, and I will clean up."

Ma started to gather the plates, but Grandma placed a hand on Ma's arm.

"Now, Liz," she said. "You're to come with us."

"Go, Mom," Dennie said.

"I will." Ma looked surprised, as if that wasn't what she had planned to say.

She went into her bedroom. We tried not to listen to Pop's loud voice. When Ma came out, her lips were tight, but she was carrying her coat.

"Be sure to get the twins to bed," she said. "We won't be very late. Grandma and Grandpa had a long trip."

We didn't see Pop for the rest of the evening. After Dennie and Molly and I got the kitchen and living room cleaned up, Bruce came over and he and Dennie went out. Molly put the twins to bed and then she dragged the phone into her room and closed the door.

It had been a stupid day, I decided. Daisy and I went to bed. I had been asleep for a couple of hours when Daisy woke me up by jumping off the bed and nosing around the door. I noticed a light coming from the kitchen and I heard the refrigerator door open and close. I wondered if Pop was looking for a piece of the mock wedding cake.

"I never was so ashamed in my life," I heard Ma say. "I would think you would be happy your mother is finding love at her age and is brave enough to go for it."

"You make it sound as if she had never been happy or in love before," Pop said. He sounded just like Anne or Alice when they're tired. "I would think one happy marriage would be enough for any woman."

"What should your mother have done, thrown herself on your father's funeral pyre?" Ma asked.

The refrigerator door closed and the kitchen light went off.

"You'd be singing a different tune if it were your mother," Pop was saying as they left the kitchen.

Daisy decided that it wasn't morning and that no one was going to let her out. She jumped back on the bed and gave me a nuzzle before she sighed and lay down.

I stared at the darkness and tried to figure out what had happened to the family since September. Back then Ma had worried that our socks matched, and that our clothes were ironed, and that we had plenty to eat. She would even make sure we'd done our homework. Now we were lucky if our socks were clean, let alone matched, and she said that if we ran our hand over our clothes when we took them from the dryer they would looked pressed.

She used to wear jeans and sweatshirts, but now she looked like an older version of Dennie. In September, Pop had just been a regular father who didn't seem to make a lot of waves, but now he was behaving the same way Molly had when the twins were born.

And then there was Grams. She had gone from being a

bossy, working grandmother to someone who started taking over our house and who now was, according to whether you talked to Ma or Pop, a gutsy little old lady who was brave enough to start a new life or a senile little old lady who was being conned by some senior Romeo.

I rested my hand gently on Daisy's head. "You're not going to go and change on me, are you?" I asked.

A deep sigh and then a slight snore were my only answer.

14

ON MONDAY OF THE NEXT WEEK, HAROLD'S daughter, Sarah Carlson, invited us to dinner on Sunday afternoon.

"You'll have to phone her to accept," Grams said. "I'd phone, but I don't think she really wants to talk to me. On Christmas Day she was anything but pleasant. You know, I could understand all this hostility if Christopher and Sarah were children, or even teenagers, but honestly, I don't understand how our getting married will make a difference to anyone. I wonder how long we can put off telling Chris about this invitation?"

After Grams left, Ma sighed and walked out of the kitchen. I heard her using the phone. She was back in a few minutes.

"What could that daughter be up to? She said she told her father to come and bring Grams at five o'clock, but she wants us to come earlier, and we're not to tell Grams."

"What do you think she's doing?" I asked.

"I'm sure I don't know." Ma groaned. "Sometimes I think I'm living in a madhouse."

I don't know how Ma explained the party to Pop, but when the two of us were alone on Friday night (everybody else but Daisy had gone shopping), Pop said to me, "You know, this daughter doesn't sound very thrilled about her father getting married, either. Maybe, between the two families, we can make them see reason. I think it's a good thing we'll be able to talk to her alone."

Fortunately, on Sunday, Grams left early to pick up Harold, so she didn't have to wonder why the rest of us were leaving at three-thirty for a five o'clock dinner.

The Carlsons lived on the other side of Golden Gate Park, where the houses are bigger and separated from each other.

"Expensive," Pop said as he parked the car. For some reason, that seemed to please him.

Mrs. Carlson opened the door. She looked like Harold, only, of course, she wasn't bald. Her hair was pulled back tight and fastened with a bunch of pins. Mr. Carlson was short and round, and the kids, a boy and a girl, were somewhere between the twins and Molly in age.

Their living room was huge. The couch stretched across almost one wall, and another wall was nothing but windows that looked out onto a garden. There were bookcases all around, and a lot of family pictures, including a photograph on the coffee table. That seemed a strange place for a picture. I stopped to look at it more carefully. It was of Harold and a woman. When I took a second look around the room, I realized that most of the photographs displayed were of Harold and this woman. Easy enough to figure out it was Harold and his first wife, the mother of Mrs. Carlson. Nice touch, I thought. The first round goes to her.

Mrs. Carlson stood in the middle of the room as if she wasn't quite sure what to do with us. "There are so many of you," she said.

We waited for her to make a choice because although the couch looked soft, it was white, and letting the twins sit on it didn't seem such a good idea. Finally Mr. Carlson brought some chairs in from the dining room. Once we were settled, Mrs. Carlson cleared her throat.

"I'm sure you're just as upset as we are. I mean, my father was perfectly happy at Cherry Garden, he was settling in, but now, ever since he met your mother, he's talking about driving again and even buying a house. Well, actually, not a house, one of those condominiums. Honestly." She looked at us. "You can't imagine how hard it was to convince him to move out of that big old house of his and to give up driving, and now, well, now." She suddenly stopped.

I thought Pop would immediately agree with her. Instead he looked puzzled. "A condominium? Why would he want to buy a condominium?"

"Why, to live in with your mother, I suppose."

"But my mother has a perfectly good house." Pop turned to Ma. "She couldn't be thinking of selling her house, could she?"

Ma shrugged. "I don't know, but why not?"

"Why not?" Pop frowned. "Because that house has been in our family for two generations, that's why."

"I knew you would agree with me," Mrs. Carlson said. "Obviously, we can't let this unsuitable arrangement continue. My father has worked hard all his life; he deserves a quiet retirement. He's not a young man."

122

Out of the corner of my eye, I saw Pop start to bristle. "Are you blaming my mother for this?" he asked. "I want you to know my mother was perfectly happy running my late father's business. She visited Cherry Garden as an act of Christian charity. My daughter Molly's class visits the patients there."

"They are not patients," Mrs. Carlson interrupted. "They are residents."

"It doesn't matter what you call them—the perception in the community is that they need cheering up. I really didn't think my mother's charitable inclinations would lead her so far afield."

There was a moment of silence as we all digested this speech. I had to give Pop credit. Whether I agreed with him or not, I really admired how he put Mrs. Carlson down.

"I must say I'm surprised. I thought we would be in total agreement on this. I never dreamed you were encouraging them," Mrs. Carlson said.

"I'm not encouraging them," Pop said. "I just want to make it perfectly clear that my mother was not the instigator of this affair. We are certainly not happy with this. But my mother was only trying to be helpful."

"Really?" asked Mrs. Carlson. "Then how do you explain her running over my father? She might have killed him."

"It was purely and simply an accident," Pop said.

"Pardon me." Dennie suddenly spoke up. "Aren't we talking about two consenting adults here? I mean, don't they have the right to do what they want? In my class—"

"Enough of that damn, pardon me, stupid class," Pop said.

"Why shouldn't Grams marry Harold?" asked Molly. "What's wrong with it?"

No one answered. Harold's two grandkids, who were sitting

on the couch facing us, began to wiggle around. I wondered if they were as embarrassed by the way their mother was acting as we were embarrassed by Pop.

"Dear," said Mrs. Carlson in a sugary-sweet voice, looking at Molly and then at Dennie, "I don't really think you or your sister is old enough to understand what the problem is."

"I guess I don't understand it either," I said.

Ma nodded her head. "I think this whole thing has been blown totally out of proportion."

"That's easy for you to say," Pop said. "Your mother and father aren't going off and getting married."

Molly snickered. "They're already married."

Pop frowned at her. "You know what I mean."

"I don't think this wrangling is getting us anywhere," Mrs. Carlson said. "The point is, what are we going to do about it?"

"Well," said Dennie, "maybe we could get a court order to stop Harold from harassing Grams. Of course," she generously added, "you could do the same."

I heard Mrs. Carlson suck in her breath. "I can certainly see where your children get their manners from," she finally said.

"Now, just a minute." Pop started to get out of his chair. "I resent that. The child was simply pointing out the fact that we can't legally prevent them from doing what they want to do. I agreed to this meeting in the hopes that between us we could think of some way of discouraging them."

I looked over to see how Dennie was taking being called a child. Not well. She was so pale all her freckles stood out like little periods on her nose, and she was waving her hand for attention as if she was in school.

At that point both Mr. Carlson and Ma started to talk.

"I think . . ." Mr. Carlson began.

"Let's just calm down," Ma said at the same time.

They both stopped and looked at each other.

"Ladies first," Mr. Carlson conceded.

"Thank you," Ma said. "The point is, it's silly to sit here arguing. You"—she nodded at both Pop and Mrs. Carlson—"have both made it abundantly clear how you feel. If they choose to get married anyway, then I think all we can do is accept it graciously. Your turn." She gestured to Mr. Carlson.

"Well put." When Mr. Carlson smiled, with his round face, he sort of looked like Santa Claus. "After all," he said, turning to his wife, "this will take some of the burden off you. You won't have to worry if your father is lonely."

Anne tugged at Ma's sleeve. "I have to go to the bathroom," she said.

From the expression on Mrs. Carlson's face, I thought she was going to deny Anne bathroom privileges. Then Mrs. Carlson sort of smiled and motioned to her daughter. "Caroline, take her . . ." she looked at Ma.

"Anne," said Ma.

"Anne," Mrs. Carlson said, "and show her where the bathroom is."

"I have to go, too," Alice said.

"Be sure you both wash your hands," Ma said.

Everyone was quiet while Anne and Alice and the Carlson kid left the room. Then Mrs. Carlson looked at her watch.

"I can see this meeting has accomplished nothing," she said. "And my father and your mother are due any minute. I had hoped we could present a united front to them, but I realize that is not going to happen."

She was obviously placing the blame for the impasse on us.

"If you'd like us to leave?" Ma offered.

"No, no, of course not, that would be too difficult to explain." Mrs. Carlson got up. "Excuse me, I have to check on the dinner."

"May I help you?" Ma asked. She was smiling, but her voice sounded the way it does when we are headed for real trouble.

"Thank you, but that won't be necessary," Mrs. Carlson said.

"Now," said Mr. Carlson, rubbing his hands, "can I get you anything? Soft drinks?" He looked at me.

I nodded. So did Dennie and Molly. Ma and Pop said they would like plain soda.

Mr. Carlson disappeared into the kitchen and Mrs. Carlson reappeared with a plate of snacks.

"They look delicious," Ma said, but she didn't take one.

In fact, none of us did. We sat in silence watching the fat on the bacon curls get hard. It was a relief when Grams and Harold arrived. They had hardly gotten their coats off before Mrs. Carlson announced dinner.

I'm not sure what happened at the dining room table because Mrs. Carlson made us eat at a "children's table" in the family room. I thought Dennie would refuse to leave the living room.

"I can't believe this," she said when she looked at the table set in the family room. "Look at this. Paper plates? Paper plates! Does she think I can't be trusted with real dishes? And Sesame Street napkins!"

I had to admit it was a bit much. Even the Carlson kids, Sam and Caroline, acted embarrassed and folded the napkins so we couldn't see Big Bird and Ernie. Sam was something of a jerk, though. His mother must have told him to play host because he kept jumping up and asking us if we wanted anything. I don't know what the grownups were eating, but we had hot dogs, beans, and carrot sticks. The twins liked them and I ate them, but Molly said she was a vegetarian (news to me) and Dennie said she never ate things with sodium nitrate in them because it was poison.

Since we had nothing in common with Sam and Caroline, agewise or anywise, things at the children's table were pretty quiet. Mrs. Carlson came in once to ask if everything was all right, but she didn't wait for an answer. The twins finished their hot dogs and scrambled down off their chairs.

"What do we do now?" they asked Sam.

Sam and Caroline looked at each other.

"Can we watch TV?" Anne asked.

"I think there's supposed to be dessert." Sam slid off his chair and went into the dining room. We could hear him talking to his mother. After a few minutes she came into the family room.

"I thought you could make your own ice cream sundaes," she said.

"I never eat ice cream. It's too fattening," Dennie said. "If you don't mind, I think I'll join the others for coffee."

Before Mrs. Carlson could react, Dennie walked into the dining room and went to stand by Grams.

Okay! I said to myself. I followed her.

"Dennie," Grams said. "Come sit down by me."

"Here, I'll get you a chair," Harold offered.

When Grams saw me, she reached up and put a hand on my arm. I felt her fingers trembling.

The dessert in this room was some kind of pudding with fruit and a caramel sauce.

"We missed you at the table," Harold said.

"Now, Father, you know how small the dining room is, and it's difficult to digest food when children are present. You did have an ulcer once."

"That was twenty years ago," Harold said. "And I don't call people in high school children." Harold motioned to Molly, who was at the kitchen door. She came in.

Mrs. Carlson didn't look very happy, but she moved some plates around and had Mr. Carlson bring the chairs in from the kitchen.

She then got into a long argument with Mr. Carlson about whether Sam and Caroline and the twins should be allowed to eat dessert with us. The discussion ended when Sam came running in and cried that one of those kids was throwing up all over the floor.

"I think," said Ma, "it's time we left."

I WAS STANDING IN FRONT OF MY LOCKER MON-
day afternoon when Molly came up to me.

"Andy?" she asked.

"What?"

"Do you think Mom and Dad will let me go to the Mardi
Gras Dance with a boy?"

The Mardi Gras Dance was an affair Bishop Alemany held
sometime between New Year's and Easter.

"They didn't let you go to that mixer. Why would they let
you go to this one? Besides, you have to have a date for this
dance," I said.

"I sort of have a date," Molly said.

"Come on," I said. "Who'd ask you?"

"If I tell you, you'll get mad."

"Why should I care who you go out with? I'm just curious
what kind of nerd would ask you."

"A lot you know," Molly said. "Martin asked me, so there."

"Martin? My Martin?"

"Since when did he become your Martin?"

"He's my friend; you can't go out with my friend," I said.

"You've got to be kidding," Molly said. "Maybe you should give me a list of every boy you know, and then I can check it before I accept a date? You're crazy!"

"Will you keep your voice down? People are looking."

"What's the matter—afraid one of your little friends might hear me?" She stalked off. I slammed the locker door. I saw Martin down the hall. "Hey, wait up," I yelled.

Martin didn't slow down. "I'm late," he called over his shoulder. "Catch you later."

Yeah, right. If I had four minutes before the next class, then so did he. So much for friendship. I didn't care if Martin dated, I told myself, but Molly? It just seemed to me it would complicate our friendship.

I was later than usual that night, but the minute I got home from school, Molly pounced on me.

"Mom and Dad want to see you," she said.

"What about?"

"About my going to the dance, and please, please, Andy, say yes."

"I don't know what you're talking about," I said. "What could I possibly have to do with your going to the dance?"

"Don't say no right off, think about it."

"What do Ma and Pop want me to do?"

Before Molly could answer, Ma came into the kitchen. "Andy, good, you're home. Your father and I want to talk to you."

"Okay," I said and waited.

"Privately."

"Okay," I said, less positively. "Where?"

"In our room."

Talk about sounding mysterious.

Pop was taking off his tie and changing out of his white shirt when Ma and I came in.

"Hi, Pop," I said.

"Hi, yourself. I want you to know this is your mother's idea. As far as I'm concerned, Molly is too young and the only reason I'm even considering it is that Martin will be her date."

I still hadn't a clue what they wanted from me.

"Ordinarily, since Molly is younger than most of the kids in her class, we would have said she was definitely too young to go to a dance with a boy," Ma said. "But since he's a friend of yours and I do know Martin's mother, that puts a slightly different light on it. And, of course, Molly is friendly with Jennie. What kind of a boy is Martin?"

"What do you mean, what kind of a boy?" I asked. "He's not a criminal, if that's what you mean, and he doesn't take drugs. You know him. You see him over here all the time."

"I know, but sometimes kids behave differently when they're around adults," Ma said.

"I don't understand. What do you want me to do, write him a character reference?"

"Don't get smart," Pop said.

"What we had in mind was your double-dating with Martin and Molly," Ma said.

"Me? What are you saying? You want me to go with them as some kind of chaperon?"

"I wouldn't put it that way," Ma said.

"Exactly how would you put it?" I asked.

"There's no reason to take that tone with your mother," Pop interrupted. "We're not asking anything so difficult."

"I don't see it that way." I lowered my voice, since Pop was beginning to look a little testy. "I mean, number one, I wasn't planning on going to this dance, and number two, even if I was, I don't have a date and," I hastily added, "I don't want one."

"You could always ask Jennie." Ma ignored my final remark.

"Martin's sister! You have got to be kidding! That girl is the worst snot I have ever met."

"Andy! That's no way to talk about a nice girl."

Nice girl my foot. I didn't say that, though.

"If you won't consider Jennie, there must be plenty of other girls in your class you could ask, or maybe one of Dennie's friends has a younger sister," Ma said.

"No way. If I agree to this idea, which I haven't, I'll find my own date."

After I said that, I realized I already sounded committed.

"I'll make a deal with you," Ma said. "If Molly agrees, you won't have to worry about the twins until summer."

"I thought my mother was watching the twins?" Pop said.

"Well, she is," Ma said. "But it never hurts to have a backup if Grams is busy or something."

I debated. Being free for the rest of the school year was certainly tempting. I had been considering going out for baseball, and now I wouldn't have to worry about late practices.

"I don't know," I finally said. "I guess I could do it if I find a girl to go with. But if I can't, that's it. No way am I going with Jennie or any of Dennie's friends' sisters. You better tell Molly what the deal is."

"I'm sure you'll have no trouble finding a girl," Ma said.

Right.

When I left the bedroom, I almost fell over Molly, who was hovering by the door.

"I assume you heard what the terms were?" I asked her. "If Grams is busy, you'll have to watch the twins."

"Thank you, thank you, thank you." For a minute I thought she was going to hug me. I backed away.

"Remember," I reminded her, "if I can't find a date, forget it."

"No sweat," Molly said. "Half the girls at school would go with anyone."

"Thanks for nothing," I said.

"I didn't mean you were anyone," Molly said. "I just meant it shouldn't be hard for you to find a date."

The next morning I hung around Martin's locker. When he saw me, he slowed down for a second and then he smiled.

"Hi, buddy," he said.

"What kind of a deal have you stuck me with?" I said.

"Hey, I'm sorry. Listen, Molly called me last night. This double-dating business wasn't my idea, but you never can tell, it might be fun."

Double-dating with Molly didn't seem like fun to me.

"We have to start going out sometime," Martin continued. "And this way, we have each other to sort of fall back on. You know, if the conversation dies. It's easier for four people to talk than two."

"I still think you should have said something to me," I said.

133

"Well, I wasn't sure how you'd feel about my dating your sister," Martin explained. "I was going to tell you eventually. I just never thought your folks would ask you to go." He stopped for a minute. "I can understand your point, though. I'd sure hate to have to double-date with Jennie."

"You see," I replied. "The only reason I agreed was because if I do it, I won't have to baby-sit the twins until summer. Now I have to find some girl to take."

The first warning bell sounded. Martin slapped me on the back. "You shouldn't have a problem," he said. "See ya."

"Sure thing," I said and headed to my alternatives to violence class. The way I figured it, my choices were pretty limited. I could only think of two possibilities: Lois, who was my partner in alternatives to violence, and Karen.

I mentally weighed the pros and cons. Lois didn't flirt with me when we did class work, but then, she might get the wrong idea if I asked her out. If she started to think we were dating, that could be a problem, since I couldn't avoid her. Besides, for all I knew, she might be dating somebody and turn me down.

On the other hand, I was pretty sure Karen would accept. She had already sort of asked me out. I considered. Could I stand Karen for a whole evening? I began to wonder if being free of the twins for four months was worth it. But then I passed the sign-up sheet for baseball. I really wanted a chance to try out. I decided one evening out of my life wouldn't be so bad. Between classes, I started looking around for Karen.

It was the last class of the day before I ran into her near the chemistry lab.

"Karen," I called. "Wait up, I want to talk to you."

"What about?" she asked, but she stopped.

I decided to be direct. "Are you going to the Mardi Gras Dance?"

She looked suspicious. "Why? Do you need somebody to watch the twins?"

She wasn't making it easy.

"Of course not," I said. "I just thought, if you weren't going, you might go with me."

"Are you asking me out, like on a date?"

"You could say that," I said.

"In other words, I get dressed up and you come over and meet my folks and we go to the dance together?"

"I thought that was the way it would go." I couldn't figure out why she was being so hostile. "If you don't want to go, just say so."

"It's not that. This just seems kind of sudden. Have you asked a whole bunch of other girls and I'm your last hope?"

"You're the only one I asked." I hoped she wouldn't take that the wrong way.

"Well, okay, then," Karen said.

"Does that mean yes?"

"What do you think?" Karen gave a long sigh.

"Fine," I said. "We're double-dating with Martin and my sister."

"Do you drive?" Karen asked.

"No, but Martin and I will work something out. You won't have to walk or take the bus, if that's what's worrying you."

"I wasn't thinking that," Karen said. "But my parents will want to know. They won't let me ride on motorcycles."

"Don't worry. I don't have a motorcycle."

"I didn't think you did, but does Martin?"

"Of course not." What did she think we were, a couple of Hell's Angels? "Don't worry. Oh, by the way, can I have your phone number?"

"Sure." She tore a piece of paper from her notebook and scribbled on it.

"Thanks," I said and shoved it in my pocket.

I heaved a sigh of relief. I'd done it. And if Karen wasn't exactly overwhelmed, neither was I. Molly would be pleased, though. I wondered how much mileage I could get out of this, aside from the baby-sitting.

GRAMS WAS THE ONLY ONE HOME WHEN I CAME in from school. She was in the living room watching TV.

"Taking it easy?" I asked.

"The twins are over at Susie's," she said. "Now that they don't have to be at that child's house, the three of them seem to get along fine."

"Isn't that always the way," I said. Grams looked sad sitting there. She didn't seem to be watching the TV, and it wasn't like Grams to be doing nothing. "You okay?" I asked.

"Yes," Grams said. "I've just been thinking."

"About something special?" I had been backing into the kitchen, but I stopped.

"Your father, Harold's daughter." She sighed and I had the sudden impulse to put my arm around her, but that would be really dopey, so I settled for sitting on the arm of the couch next to her.

137

"I think it's crummy how Pop has been about Harold," I said.

"Yes, well," Grams said. "I guess nothing is as easy as it seems. But it's obvious after that disastrous dinner party that there's no point pretending everyone will eventually get along. Harold and I have talked about what to do. Harold wants to elope."

"Elope!" I exclaimed. I immediately pictured Harold, in the middle of the night, trying to get Grams down a ladder. Actually, the only window open to the street was in the room that Ma and Pop now had as their bedroom. "Would you do such a thing?"

"No, I think that would be a little out of character for me. I'm too old to run away. I want to get married in a church with my family present." She laughed. "Listen to me. You'd think I was Dennie's age. Don't look so serious, Andy, it's not the end of the world. Harold and I will still be friends, and at our age I think we can live with that arrangement. Harold should move out of Cherry Garden, though, it's not really the place for him, but other than that, when my house is finished, I'll go back there alone."

I felt terrible. "Will you open up the gallery again?" I asked.

"I don't think so," Grams said. "I just don't seem to have the heart for it anymore. Maybe I'll sell the house and find a smaller place."

"Gee, Grams, is there something I can do?" I asked.

"No, dear, but you're sweet. I'm glad we're alone. There's something I want you to have. My engagement ring." She slipped a ring off her finger, took my hand, and laid the ring on my palm.

"Grams!" I said. "I can't take this. Shouldn't this be Dennie's? I mean, if you don't want to keep it?"

"No, I'm leaving the girls all the rest of my jewelry, but this was your great-grandmother's engagement ring and your grandfather gave it to me and I want you to give it to the girl you marry."

I almost laughed. Getting married was something so far from my mind, I couldn't even imagine it.

Grams shook her head. "I know right now that seems like a pretty silly idea, but that's all right. Put it in a safe place and someday you may want to use it. There's no deadline, so don't feel I'm rushing you."

"But if you and Harold aren't getting married," I said, "I mean, won't you still need your ring?"

"Harold has already given me a ring. It's not as fancy as this one, and now I guess I can consider it a pledge of friendship, but I wouldn't feel right wearing my old one anymore. I think it's time I took it off and gave it to the next generation."

I didn't want to remind her that the next generation was really Pop. In a way, I was proud she wanted me to have it, but the whole idea of an engagement ring sitting in my drawer kind of spooked me. It was like I was already grownup.

The front door slammed and I heard Molly's and Dennie's voices.

I put the ring in my pocket. "Gee, Grams, I don't know what to say."

"You don't have to say anything. Particularly to your father."

"Right."

"And, Andy, if the girl you decide to marry doesn't like the ring—I know fashions change and some people don't like wearing other people's things—don't worry. She doesn't have to take it. It's okay if you sell it. Family and traditions are all well and good, but not when they get in the way of living."

"Thanks, Grams" was all I could think of to say. But I thought to myself that any girl I might consider marrying had better like this ring or she'd be all washed up in my book.

"You're a good grandson," Grams said. "I'm lucky to have such a nice one." She got up and left the living room. In a few minutes I heard her bedroom door close.

For the first time in years and years, I felt like crying.

Daisy wandered out from the kitchen and nosed around my hand. I reached down and patted her head. Families! I went into the kitchen, opened the refrigerator, and pulled out a carton of milk. I found a glass and poured some milk into it. I stood at the sink staring down at the glass. "It's not fair," I said to Daisy, who had followed me. Suddenly the sight of the white foaming liquid made me nauseated. I poured it into the sink. There must be something I can do, I thought. Except I didn't have a clue.

Molly wandered in. "Why are you staring at the sink? Is it stopped up?" She peered into it. "It looks okay to me. Have you found a date?"

"What?"

"A date, an arrangement for two people to go out together. What's the matter with you? Have you forgotten about your promise?" Molly asked.

"Oh, yeah." Amazing! My date with Karen had slipped my mind.

"Well, have you found a date?"

"No sweat. Didn't you think I could do it?"

"Who's the girl?"

"Nobody you know." I shoved my hands into my pocket and was starting toward my room when I felt Grams's ring. I stopped and turned around. "Say, Molly, have you talked to Grams?"

"Grams? Sure, I talk to her all the time. About anything in particular?"

"She just told me she and Harold aren't going to get married."

"You're kidding!"

"Why would I kid about that?" I asked. "Listen, Molly, I'm serious. Grams feels terrible."

"What happened?"

"Nothing in particular. I mean nothing new. I think that dinner party was the last straw."

"Poor Grams," Molly said. "Maybe Dennie has an idea of what we can do. She's in our room. Come on."

I followed Molly to her bedroom.

"Have you heard Grams and Harold aren't getting married?" Molly announced as she opened the door.

Dennie was on her hands and knees, her head in the closet. She turned around, and when she saw me she frowned. "What do you want?"

"Only visiting," I joked.

"It's okay," Molly said. She bounced onto her bed.

I was surprised. Their room looked worse than mine. There were clothes all over the beds and floor and most of the drawers were half-open, with bits and pieces of material hanging out. The top of Dennie's bureau was full of bottles and jars. Molly's was covered with books and school stuff. Her typewriter was wedged between the mirror and her knapsack.

"Did they have a fight?" Dennie asked.

I shook my head. "It's because of the way Pop and Harold's daughter are acting. Grams is really depressed."

"This is all wrong," Dennie declared, resting back on her heels. "I don't know why they don't go ahead and get married anyway."

Nobody asked me, but I sat down on the edge of Dennie's bed. "Harold wants to elope, but Grams said no, she'd settle for being friends." I shrugged. "I guess there's nothing we can do about it."

"Don't you care whether Grams is happy or not?" Dennie asked.

"Of course I care," I said. I really did. Grams deserved to be happy. Except I couldn't see what we could do about it. Pop and Mrs. Carlson were causing the problem. I said as much to Dennie.

"If we all felt like you, we'd be in a fine mess," Dennie said.

"What's that supposed to mean?"

"It means you have to do something for others. People have to take care of other people."

"You sound like you've taken too many religion classes," I said. "How does this help Grams?"

"We have to convince Grams it's okay to marry. That Dad will eventually come around."

"I don't think talking will do much good. Pop won't listen to us," I said. "Talking won't solve anything."

"You know, Andy, in your own crazy way you may be right," Dennie said after a minute.

"Right about what?"

"About doing something. We can help them elope. You said Harold wants to, that he just agreed to be friends to keep Grams happy."

"Elope? Elope where?" Molly asked.

"That's stupid," I said. "What are they going to do, run away to Reno?"

"Of course," Dennie said. "You see, Andy, you can be smart. Reno is perfect. It's close, and there's no waiting period or blood test. We learned that in my marriage class."

142

"But Grams wants to be married in church, she said so, and she wants all of us with her," I said.

"But don't you see," Dennie said, "we can go with them. You and me and Molly and Bruce."

"Why Bruce?" I interrupted.

"Because it's a long drive, and besides he'd like to go. Leave it to me. Come on, we'll talk to her right now," Dennie said.

"My goodness," Grams said when she opened her door and saw the three of us standing there. "What's the occasion?"

"Grams, can we come in?" Dennie said.

"Of course." Grams opened the door wider.

Once we were inside, Dennie said, "Grams, we think you should marry Harold."

Grams looked at me.

"You didn't tell me not to tell anyone," I said.

"It doesn't matter," Grams replied. "And it's sweet of you to care, Dennie, but really, it's all for the best."

"But, Grams, you and Harold love each other," Molly protested.

"Now, you children aren't to worry. Harold and I have decided that we would feel terribly guilty if we were to cause our families any unhappiness. I couldn't sleep at night knowing your father hated Harold, and Harold feels the same way about his daughter and me. So we've decided to be friends and let it go at that."

"Dad would get used to it. He's gotten used to Bruce, and he couldn't stand him at first," Dennie said.

"That may be," Grams said. "Although I can't say he's exactly embraced Bruce with open arms, but this is different."

"We agree with Harold, we think you should elope," Molly said. "It will be fun. We can leave at night. How long does it take to get to Reno anyway?"

"Reno?" Grams exclaimed. "Why would you want me to get married in Reno?"

"It's close by, and we're going to help you." Dennie took one of Grams's hands. "Bruce and I will drive you, and Andy and Molly will come along for moral support. You see, it won't be complicated at all."

"But I want to be married by a priest," Grams said. "Even though Harold's not a Catholic, he respects my feelings."

"I told you," I said.

Dennie gave me a dirty look. "Shut up," she said.

"Now, Dennie," Grams interrupted. "It's a sweet but totally impractical idea."

"No, it's not. You can be married by a priest. I'll talk to Father Tavernetti," Dennie said. "You know, there are such things as dispensations about getting married in a different state. I know he can help us."

"Father Tavernetti?" I said. "That's the principal. You would just ask him to do something like that?"

"Why not?" Dennie asked. "I did a piece on him for the newspaper, and we got to be pretty good friends. So." Dennie patted Grams's hand. "Trust us. Everything will work out great."

"I'll have to talk to Harold," Grams said. "You have to give me time to think."

I was glad Grams wasn't rushing into anything. I wanted Grams to be happy, but Dennie's idea sounded insane. Besides, Pop would kill us.

"I don't want you children to get into trouble over me," Grams cautioned.

"Grams, there won't be any trouble," Dennie assured her. "You'll see. Talk to Harold and then start looking for a wedding dress. I'll help you."

144

I swear, Grams blushed and giggled.

"Are you sure this is a good idea?" I asked Dennie as we went back to her room.

"Sure," she said. "Why not?"

"I can't put my finger on it," I replied, "but I think there's a fatal flaw here somewhere. Pop's not going to like it for one, and then, what right do we have meddling in something we don't understand?"

"What don't you understand?" Molly asked. "Maybe I can explain it to you."

"Very funny," I said.

"We're not meddling, we're helping them do what they want," Dennie explained. "And as far as Dad goes, I don't think he'll do anything once it's all over. You know him. Once something has happened, he adjusts."

"I hope you're right," I said.

"I think blush lace would be pretty on Grams," Dennie said to Molly.

"I can wear the dress I get for the dance," Molly said.

I left. Talking about what to wear when we were planning a major mutiny was crazy.

THE IDEA OF HELPING GRAMS ELOPE BOTHERED ME. A little voice inside me said we should leave it to the adults. I was also blown away by the idea of Dennie actually asking the principal to help her just as if they were friends. Students and principals are never friends. And besides, what right did he have to know what was going on in our family?

"Stop worrying," I told myself. Probably nothing will come of it. I was wrong. When I got home from school the next day, there was a note from Grams inviting the three of us to dinner at Tía Teresa, a Mexican restaurant. She had gone to pick up Harold and would swing by at six-thirty to get us.

"A planning meeting," Molly declared. "What do you bet they want to set a date?"

"You're right," Dennie said.

"I say they want to thank us for caring, but no thanks," I said.

Ma was surprised when she heard we would all be gone for dinner.

Grams and Harold picked us up at six twenty-five. We crammed ourselves into the back seat of Grams's car. Harold was driving.

"So," Harold said, "I understand we're going on a trip."

"I knew you'd do it," Molly cried. "When are we going?"

"We'll talk about that," Grams said. "I don't want you children missing any school. And then we have to consider Bruce's schedule. Oh, dear, I forgot to ask you to invite him. Dennie, I'm sorry."

"Don't worry," Dennie said. "He's working tonight."

Harold slowed down as he got near the restaurant, and when he spotted a parking spot, he zipped into it on one try.

"Wow!" Dennie said. "You can really park. I couldn't have gotten into a place that size."

"Anybody can park better than you can," I said.

"I love driving," Harold said. "I was crazy to let my daughter talk me into selling my car."

Harold leaped out and ran around the car to open the door for Grams.

"Now, that's polite," Dennie said to me. "I hope you're this polite when you're out with Karen."

"What about all your big talk about women being equal?" I said. I climbed out of the car but didn't hold open the door for Molly and Dennie.

"Doesn't hurt to make a woman feel special," Harold said to me, and then he held the door open for them.

Once we were seated in the restaurant and had ordered dinner, Grams and Harold smiled at us.

"This is so wonderful of you children," Grams said. "Harold and I won't forget it."

"Yes," Harold agreed. "When Louise told me what you wanted to do, I realized there was hope after all." He chuckled. "And Reno. Shades of Hollywood."

"Besides," Grams said, "there won't be any chance of Sarah or Christopher's finding out until it's too late. I just hope you're right, Dennie, and your father will accept the done deed."

"I want Bruce to be my best man," Harold said.

"He'll love to," Dennie said promptly.

"And you're to be my maid of honor." Grams patted Dennie's hand. "And you, Molly, will be my bridesmaid."

I figured I was just going along for the ride when Grams looked at me. "And I want you to give me away, Andy."

"Gee, Grams," I said.

"I know I'm going to a lot of fuss, but I want this to be special."

Harold leaned over and kissed her lightly on the cheek. "It will be special."

For a minute the rest of us got very busy with our napkins and water glasses. Finally I asked the burning question. "Exactly how are we going to do this without Pop and Ma knowing? Won't they be suspicious if we all just leave?"

"That's why we're here," Molly said. "To plan the details. I could say I was spending the night at Jennie's."

"Oh, dear," Grams said. "I don't want you lying. No."

"I won't have to lie exactly," Molly said. "I could carry my backpack and say I was going over to Jennie's and that I'd be home late the next day. Mom and Dad could draw their own conclusions."

"No." Grams was definite. "Harold and I don't want to start our new life with a lie."

"What about the rest of us?" I said. "I guess Dennie could say her store was taking inventory all night, but I can't think of any reason to leave the house."

"Don't make it so difficult," Dennie said. "It's simple. Mom and Dad go to bed at eleven. At midnight we sneak out. Bruce can pick us up a block away so they won't hear his car. Grams can leave a note. I don't see any problem at all. It only takes five hours or so to drive to Reno. By the time Mom and Dad read the note, it will be too late for them to do anything."

"Sounds good to me," Molly said. "Now all we have to do is decide on a date."

"Any weekend is fine with me," I said. "I have nothing planned."

"Yes you have." Molly gave me a punch. "We can't go two weeks from now. It's the dance."

"You can't miss that," Grams said.

"That's too soon, anyway," Dennie said. "Father Tavernetti said his friend in Reno would need a couple of weeks at least to arrange the dispensation."

"Is a month time enough?" Molly asked. "We'll be off for Easter vacation then, and we can go in the middle of the week."

"That sounds good," Dennie said. "Except there's a sale planned toward the end of the week. Maybe we could leave Easter night? That way I can still work at the sale."

"Four weeks will be perfect," Grams said. "It gives me a chance to settle the plans for my house and more time to find a dress."

"I won't have to rent a tux, will I?" Harold asked.

"No," Grams replied. "At my age I'm not wearing a white dress or a veil. Now, let's enjoy our dinner."

This plan made me feel very nervous. I couldn't understand how everybody seemed to think this idea would work. I tried to talk to Molly about it once when we were the only ones home.

"If they're going to get married, why don't they just do it?" I asked. "Why all this business of running off to Reno?"

"Because it's so romantic," Molly said. "And because unless Grams moved back to her house, Dad could get suspicious. You just don't show up at church and ask to get married. Grams and Harold would have to get blood tests and licenses and make arrangements with the priest. Dennie explained all this to me. But if they elope, Dad won't get a chance to suspect anything. Besides, I think Harold likes doing something as exciting as this."

I guess it made sense, but I was relieved it was a month away. Anything can happen in a month. So I ignored it when Dennie and Molly and Grams would go into her room and shut the door. The less I knew, the happier I was, and, anyway, I was too busy worrying about my date with Karen. I had the feeling she didn't even like me very much. Suppose she accepted the date to embarrass me because she was mad that I didn't go to her party? Then there was the problem of dancing. I could hardly make it across the floor without falling down. The more I thought, the more I worried and the more nervous I got.

On the Wednesday before the Saturday dance, Martin said, "My sister Maggie will drive us to the dance. Can Dennie pick us up?"

"I guess," I replied. I had thought Molly would take care of details like that.

"When will you know?" Martin persisted.

"It's only Wednesday. What are you so excited about?"

"I don't know," Martin said. "Thank God there'll be the two of us."

"You've got it easy," I said. "You won't have to talk at all. Molly never shuts up. How about me? I don't know this Karen at all."

"We have to get our times straight," Martin continued. "What time did you tell Karen you'd pick her up?"

"I haven't thought about that," I said. Details, details. They can drive a person crazy.

"The dance starts at nine," Martin said. "So we have to decide on when to arrive. Where does Karen live?"

I shook my head.

"Well, find out. We don't want to be the first ones at the dance, we'd look too eager. Maggie says nobody ever arrives when the dance starts. And you'll have to talk to her parents, so we need to take that into consideration."

"I forgot about having to talk to her parents. What am I supposed to talk about?" I asked. "I don't even know what I'm going to say to Karen."

"That's your problem," Martin said. "Depending on where she lives and how bad traffic is, I think we should plan on getting to the dance around nine-thirty. So call Karen, find out where she lives, and once you find that out, you can tell her what time we'll pick her up."

I nodded. I guess it made sense.

"Phone her tonight and then phone me so I can tell Maggie what the schedule is."

"Sure, sure," I said.

When I got home, I grabbed the phone before I lost my nerve. I was disconcerted when Karen didn't answer. Girls always answer the phone. Even if Ma and Pop are sitting in the living room, if the phone rings, Ma is always the one to get it.

A male voice said, "Hello."

I gulped. "Where's Karen? I mean, can I talk to Karen?"

"Why?"

I realized I was talking to a kid.

"It's about school, put her on."

I heard the receiver bang down and the kid yelling, "Karen, some android wants to talk to you."

"Shut up," Karen yelled back.

I waited. Finally the receiver was picked up.

"Hello?"

"Karen?" I asked.

"Yes?"

"It's me, Andy. I'm calling about the dance on Saturday."

"Are you calling it off?" she asked.

"Of course not. Why would you think such a thing? I need to know where you live."

I listened to her directions. She didn't live very far away, and I decided it would be better to be late than early. It would leave less time to talk. "I'll pick you up at nine-fifteen."

"Fine," Karen said.

"Goodbye," I said.

I leaned against the wall and used the tail of my shirt to dry my hands. When Molly wandered by, she asked, "What are you waiting for, the phone to dial itself?"

"Can it. And you can phone Martin and tell him we'll pick up Karen at nine-fifteen."

At dinner, Ma asked me, "Are you getting Karen flowers?"

"I told Martin to get me flowers," Molly said. "He said he'd order one for you, too."

"I hope you told him not to spend a fortune," I said.

152

"Don't be so cheap," Molly said.

"Molly!" exclaimed Grams. "You don't tell a boy to bring you flowers!"

"Well, why not? I mean, maybe he wouldn't know he was supposed to and then he'd be embarrassed."

"Good for you," Dennie said. "If you don't tell people what you want, they'll never know. People don't like guessing games."

Pop grunted.

When I woke up Saturday morning, I rolled over and looked at Daisy. She thumped her tail, stood up and balanced on my legs, and proceeded to stretch.

"You know," I said, "you've got it made. You don't have to worry about how to talk to the spaniel down the street."

Daisy dropped off the bed and pawed at the door. I leaned over and opened it for her. Molly was in the kitchen.

"What are you doing up so early?" I asked, getting out of bed.

"I'm nervous," she said. "Do you always sleep in your gym shorts? No wonder they're such a mess."

"Why shouldn't I?" I pushed the door closed, picked up my jeans, and put them on over the shorts. Then I went into the kitchen.

"What are you nervous about?" I asked, opening the refrigerator and pulling out a carton of milk.

"Aren't you nervous?" she asked. "It's your first date, too."

I shrugged. "No big deal." I wasn't going to give her the satisfaction of knowing my real thoughts.

"Suppose I step on Martin's feet. Suppose we fall on the dance floor?"

I didn't answer her. Instead, I poured cereal in a bowl and spooned sugar over it.

"I'm not a good dancer. Bruce tried to teach me and I stepped all over his feet," Molly continued.

"Are you going to do something with your hair?" I asked, changing the subject.

"Why? Are you afraid I'll embarrass you? Of course I'm going to do something with my hair. Dennie's going to fix it. How does Karen wear her hair?"

I tried to think of her hair. To be honest, I couldn't even remember what color it was.

"Do you know what Karen's wearing?" Molly said.

I hadn't thought to ask. "Why do I need to know that?"

"I guess it doesn't matter," Molly said. "I told Martin he should get you some white flowers to give her. Do you think Karen will wear high heels? How tall is she?"

I desperately tried to remember if I had to look up, down, or straight ahead when I talked to her. Oh, well, I thought. Girls notice things like that. Karen would know if she should wear high heels.

Ma and Dennie came in from their run and they started talking about stupid things, so I put my bowl in the dishwasher, the milk in the refrigerator, and the cereal box in the cabinet and wandered back to my room to get properly dressed. I squinted into the mirror over my bureau and tried to decide if the shadow on my face was the start of a beard or just bad lighting. I ran my hand over my cheek. It wouldn't hurt to take the electric razor out for a run. I pulled it out of the drawer, unplugged my lamp, and plugged it in. I was surprised how noisy it was.

I quickly turned it off. I decided to wait until I was alone before I practiced with it.

"Andy." Molly banged on my door. "A girl wants to talk to you."

"What? A girl's here?"

"No, dummy, on the phone. If you weren't making so much noise playing with that dumb razor, you'd have heard the phone ringing."

"Shut up," I said. I went to get the phone.

"Hello?" I asked.

"I can't go," a girl's voice told me.

I didn't recognize the voice; it sounded muffled and shaky.

"Who is this?" I asked.

"Who do you think? It's Karen."

"You sound funny. Is something wrong?" I then realized what she had said. "You can't go? Why can't you go?"

"Because I have seven chicken pox on my stomach, no, make that eight, and five on my face."

"Chicken pox!"

"You don't have to shout," Karen said. "And I have two inside my mouth, which is why I'm talking funny. I'm sorry."

"Yeah, well, that's okay." I couldn't think of anything else to say, so I hung up. I wondered if that was rude. Maybe I should have said I was sorry, except I'm not a very good liar.

IT TOOK ME A MINUTE TO REALIZE THAT I WAS
saved. I was free. I didn't have to go to the dance. Surely Ma
and Pop would still let Molly and Martin go, but even if they
didn't, that wasn't my problem. I certainly hadn't given Karen
the chicken pox. I think something like that was called an act
of God. Thank you, God.

"Hey, Molly," I yelled. "Come here."

"What?" Molly came into the hall.

"That was Karen on the phone. She can't go to the dance,
she has the chicken pox."

"Chicken pox!" Molly screamed. "She can't do that to me.
Maybe she can cover them up?"

"I don't think so." I tried to sound disappointed.

"Maybe we won't have to tell Mom and Dad," Molly
suggested. "If you leave the house with us, they'll never know
you aren't going to pick up Karen."

"And what am I supposed to do while you're at the dance?"

"You can go to the movies or something," Molly said.

"No thanks."

"I'll talk to Mom," Molly said. "She should certainly understand this wasn't my fault."

"Go for it." I decided the farther away from that discussion I was, the better. I got Daisy's leash from the hall closet and jingled it. "Walk, Daisy," I called.

Daisy came skidding into the hallway, tongue hanging out. I snapped the leash on her collar and we left the house. I found myself whistling. I felt as if I had arrived at class to take a final and the teacher had said that there was no test and everybody had gotten an A.

"Race you to the corner," I challenged Daisy. She woofed and started loping down the street, stretching the leash tight. "Atta girl," I yelled.

I was humming when I went back into the house.

"Why are you so cheerful?" Pop demanded when I met him in the hallway.

"It's Saturday," I said.

Pop just made a noise in his throat and started to go through my room to the garage. "This room is a disgrace," he said. "Better start clearing it out if you want to go to that dance tonight."

"No sweat."

"Don't get fresh." He slammed my door.

I wondered how long Molly was going to put off telling them. I could understand her strategy. They could hardly refuse to let her go if Martin was practically at the door.

I had planned on worrying all day and imagining the worst things that could happen on a date so that I would be prepared for anything, but now that I didn't have to worry, I was at loose ends. I could write my paper for my violence class. But when I tried to sit down and think, my feet wouldn't stay still. I could go to Martin's, but I didn't see any reason to get him upset before it was necessary. Besides, telling him was Molly's job. Finally I grabbed my jacket and yelled at Ma that I would be at St. Edward's shooting a few baskets. There were always kids hanging around the playground trying to drum up a game of sudden death.

By the time I got home, it was dinner. Apparently, Molly had finally broken the news, because Ma was trying to talk Dennie and Bruce into double-dating. "I really don't under-stand why you and Bruce can't go," she was saying to Dennie.

"Please, Mother, we've gone over this a hundred times. Judy is giving a party. It's a celebration for her boyfriend who just got accepted at some college back East. I don't mind leaving the party for a while to pick up Martin and Molly and bring them home." She turned to Molly. "You guys better be ready. But"—she turned back to Ma—"I'm not going to miss the whole party. Besides, seniors don't go to this dance." She saw that I was about to say something. "I don't know why seniors don't go; that's not the point. I thought we were doing everybody a big favor by agreeing to pick them up."

"Well, it's too late to make any changes now, anyway," Ma conceded. "I guess it will work out all right."

Martin came over about eight forty-five. He was dressed in slacks and a sport coat and carried two boxes with the name of a florist on the lids. He gave one box to Molly and one to me.

"Molly phoned me about Karen, but the owner said it was too late to cancel. You owe me twelve ninety-five, but if you don't want to pay, I'll understand. You were doing me a favor."

"Of course he'll pay you," Ma said. She gave me a dirty look. I took the box.

"Thanks," I said. "I'll give you the money on Monday."

Molly acted so excited when she got hers that she seemed incapable of untying the gold cord.

"Here." Martin took the box out of her hand. "Let me help you."

Molly made a big deal of slipping the flowers onto her wrist. Then Ma took a picture of Martin and Molly.

As they started out the door, Martin grabbed my arm. "Are you sure you don't want to come along? I won't mind."

"I'll pass," I said.

Once they were gone, Ma looked at the box still in my hand. "I guess you better put it in the refrigerator."

"I suppose." I took off the cord and opened the lid and looked at the corsage. There was a small cluster of white blossoms of some kind with a small pink rose in the middle.

"It's not very big for twelve ninety-five," I said.

"Flowers aren't cheap. And it's small because it's meant to be worn at the wrist," Ma explained. "It's a shame Karen won't see it. If she didn't have something like the chicken pox, you could have given it to her at school Monday."

Right! Catch me handing a girl flowers in front of half the student body.

"Such a waste," Ma continued. "You could take it over to Karen's. That is, if you want to. I mean, it's strictly up to you."

Talk about guilt trips. I thought for a minute. The flowers were no good to me, and girls seemed to like that kind of stuff. Why not? "Okay," I said. "I'll take them over to her."

"Do you want me to drive you?"

"I'll go on my bike," I said.

I went down to the garage. It took me almost fifteen minutes to find my bike, since Pop had rearranged the dining room furniture again. I used to ride all the time when I was at St. Edward's, but since I'd graduated, I think my bike has only been out a few times. The bike was dusty and the front tire was soft, but not completely flat. I wheeled it out the side door.

Karen's house looked a lot like ours, with the garage level with the sidewalk. I parked my bike in a dark corner near the front stairs and hoped no one would steal it. It was such a mess, though, I figured it was probably safe.

Karen's mother opened the door.

I cleared my throat. "I'd like to see Karen," I said.

Her mother looked at the flower box in my hand. "You must be Andy."

I nodded.

"You've had the chicken pox?"

"Yes."

She opened the door completely. "Come on in and sit down. I'll get Karen." That was the last time I saw her. I could hear her talking to Karen, and they seemed to be arguing. I began to wish I hadn't come.

Finally Karen showed up. "Don't look at me." She sounded as if she had pebbles in her mouth. "I feel like one giant zit."

I swallowed hard. Don't look at me? What was I supposed to do, keep my eyes closed and shove the box at her?

"You can open your eyes, stupid, I didn't mean you had to keep them closed. I just don't want you staring at me."

It was pretty dark in the living room, since Karen hadn't turned on any lights.

"You don't look so bad," I said. Actually, from what I could see, she looked pretty gross.

She moved closer and sat down on the edge of the couch. "Honestly?" she asked.

160

"You should have seen my twin sisters when they had them. Anne even got them up her nose."

Karen shivered. "That's disgusting." She raised one hand as if to scratch and then put it down. "Mom says if I scratch I'll have scars. That's all I need. I'm sorry about the dance, but I honestly didn't know I had them until this morning. All I had yesterday was a crummy headache. If I had known earlier, you could have asked somebody else."

Thank God she hadn't known. "Don't worry about it," I said. Then I remembered the box in my hand. "Here." I pushed it along the couch toward her.

She picked up the box and opened it and took out the flowers. She stretched the elastic over her hand and held up her arm. "They're beautiful," she said. "You shouldn't have. I mean, I know you must have ordered them, but you could have told the florist you wouldn't take them."

I almost said that it had been too late to cancel, but then I thought of Dennie telling me how insensitive I am. I didn't say anything; I just smiled in what I hoped was a sensitive way.

"I couldn't believe it when I looked in the mirror and saw spots. At first I thought I had a rash from nerves, but Mom took one look and said, 'Chicken pox.' " Then Karen added, "My folks wouldn't let me go out on dates last year, so this would have been my first dance. I guess you've had lots of dates and weren't worried?"

I started to nod my head and then I thought, what the heck. With Karen sitting there in the dark covered with chicken pox, wearing jeans and a T-shirt, it didn't seem right to play games with her.

"No," I confessed. "This would have been my first dance, too. And I was worried about having things to talk about."

"Were you really? You know, I made a list of subjects so if

161

the silence went on too long, I wouldn't have to think. I could just sneak a look at my list."

"My friend Martin, who we were double-dating with, thought it would help that there would be four of us. That way, somebody would be sure to think of something to say," I said.

"What will Martin and Molly do now?" Karen asked.

"Oh, Molly has no trouble talking."

"It was awfully nice of you to let your sister and her date come with us. Most boys aren't nice to their younger sisters at all. My older brother who's in college wouldn't even be seen on the same side of the street with me."

I dismissed the compliment with a vague smile.

"Would you like a Pepsi or Coke?" Karen stood up.

"Whatever," I said.

She left and I was alone in the living room, which was now completely dark. When she came back, she was carrying a tray with two full glasses and a plate of cookies.

"They're safe. I didn't touch them, so they don't have any germs on them." She put the tray on the coffee table and leaned over and turned on one of the lamps.

I took a cookie and a glass.

"Are you disappointed you didn't go to the dance?" Karen asked.

"Not really."

"Why did you ask me if you didn't want to go?"

I thought a minute. No matter what I said, it all sounded sort of insulting to Karen. "Well, it's not as if it's the only dance I'll ever go to," I finally said.

That seemed to satisfy her. "You know," she said, "you're a lot nicer than I thought you'd be."

162

"If you didn't think I was nice, why did you agree to go out with me?" I asked.

"You never know," Karen said.

I wasn't sure what that meant, but I decided to let it ride. It appeared to me we were both using each other. In a way, that seemed fair. You have to start somewhere.

NOW THAT I COULD STOP WORRYING ABOUT Karen, I started thinking about the elopement. All along, I kept hoping it would be one of those things that people just talk about and never do. But it soon became obvious that I was the only one who wasn't taking the plan seriously.

When Dennie told me that the dispensation had gone through and Father Owens in Reno was sending Grams and Harold the paperwork to fill out, I knew that on the Monday after Easter, I was going to be standing in a church in Reno watching my grandmother get married.

"We'll leave at midnight Easter Sunday and arrive in Reno early in the morning," Grams explained. "Harold and I have booked a hotel room. You children can use it if you like while Harold and I get our license and visit Father Owens. We can use the hotel room to change our clothes and then we'll get married and have a nice meal, and if there's a decent early show, maybe we can see it, and then we'll drive home." She paused for breath and fanned her face with her hand.

"You and Harold should stay over," Dennie said. "You could fly home later. Give yourself a little honeymoon."

"Harold and I couldn't do that," Grams said. "We wouldn't leave you children to brave the wrath of your father alone, or of Sarah, either."

Dennie laughed and leaned over to give Grams a hug.

When Grams wasn't there, I asked, "So we're really going to do this?"

"Of course we are," Dennie said. "You're not chickening out, are you? Listen, if you don't want to go, don't. We can get along without you."

"No, I said I was going and I am." I remembered Grams's engagement ring sitting in a drawer next to the electric razor. Having it in my drawer made me feel somehow committed to supporting Grams and wanting to see her happy.

The last Saturday before Easter week, Grams asked me if I wanted to go over to her house and help her clean it up.

"Are you planning to move back?" Ma asked. She looked over her shoulder to see if Pop was listening. He wasn't.

"Oh, I don't think the house is completely ready yet." Grams managed to look vague. "I'm taking Molly and Dennie, too," she added.

"Goodness," Ma said. "What are you doing?"

"I might want to move things around," Grams explained.

When she went to get her coat, Molly leaned over and whispered to me, "What do you think she's up to?"

I hadn't realized she was up to anything.

Grams stopped at Cherry Garden to pick up Harold before we crossed the Bay Bridge and headed toward Alameda.

"We are going to my house," Grams said to us. "I didn't lie to your parents, but Harold and I want you to see the condo we bought."

"Why aren't you going to live in your house?" Molly asked.

"We decided all those stairs were just asking for trouble," Grams said. "It was only a matter of time before one of us breaks our neck on them."

"Are you going to sell your house?" Dennie asked.

"No, Vivian has been renting a terrible house, and since Harold and I want to do some traveling but we'd like to keep the business, we decided to make Vivian a partner and she can live in the house. I think it should work out very well."

"I knew I was marrying someone beautiful, but I never realized your grandmother was such a sharp businesswoman." Harold gave Grams a quick kiss on the cheek.

"Please, Harold, not while I'm driving," Grams said, but she didn't look angry.

When we finished packing the car with boxes from Grams's house, Harold drove us over to their new home. It was in a complex of condominiums that were built close to the Alameda shoreline.

"Come out to the deck," Harold said. "We can see right across the bay to San Francisco."

"Isn't it beautiful?" Grams stood next to Harold, her arm linked with his. Her eyes glowed. I sighed and decided maybe we were doing the right thing.

Grandpa and Grandma Reid always come up for Easter brunch. They planned to do the same this year. Fortunately, there's some kind of traditional mobile-home owners' rally in Oregon right after Easter, so they always leave early Easter afternoon. We wouldn't have to worry about them keeping Ma and Pop up late talking.

Grams treated us to Easter brunch at the Fairmont Hotel. Harold wasn't there. They must have decided it would make everyone less suspicious if they weren't together. It didn't work. Grandma kept trying to talk about the wedding, and what plans Grams and Harold had made. Grams just said that there were some problems.

"Problems? Problems?" Grandpa roared. "Nonsense, I'm sure it's only a lovers' spat."

"My mother is aware whether she is having second thoughts," Pop said through clenched teeth.

"Just remember, at our age, we can't afford to dilly-dally around," Grandpa said. Grandma tugged at his sleeve, so after that remark, he didn't say much else.

After the brunch, Grandpa and Grandma drove off to Oregon and Grams went to her room.

"Do you think her feelings are hurt?" Ma asked no one in particular. "I don't know what gets into Grandpa. He never knows when to stop teasing."

"Maybe she's just tired," Dennie said, and then she and Molly went to their room.

"If they hadn't already had the chicken pox, I'd think they were coming down with it," Ma said. "Dennie looks as if she's running a fever. How do you feel?"

"Fine," I said. Somebody had to keep up appearances, so that Ma and Pop didn't get suspicious.

Ma made a lunch sort of dinner and we stood around the table and picked at it. It wasn't even worth sitting down for. Pop took his sandwich into the living room and turned on the

TV. The twins, full of Easter candy and the late brunch, whined and said they weren't hungry.

"What's the matter with everybody?" Ma finally asked. "You are all so quiet. Has something happened that you don't want to tell us about?"

Grams put down her sandwich. "I have a slight headache. Maybe I drank too much coffee at the hotel. If no one minds, I think I'll turn in."

When Grams left, Ma turned to the rest of us. "Before you wander off, please decide who will be minding the twins next week. Since you're out of school, it's not fair to expect Grams to watch them."

From the expression on Dennie's and Molly's faces, I think they had forgotten about the twins.

"You guys sort it out." I reached for another sandwich. "In case anyone has forgotten, I'm out of the loop."

Molly looked at me. "That doesn't seem quite fair," she said. "After all, you didn't do anything."

"Breaks of the game," I said.

"I'm not going to worry about it," Dennie declared after Ma left the kitchen. "Dad can stay home tomorrow. If he wasn't behaving like such a nut, we wouldn't have to do this."

I knew Dennie was right, but I took the long view. One more reason for Pop to kill us.

THE EVENING DRAGGED ON, BUT FINALLY MA AND
Pop went to bed. I gathered up my good slacks and sweater
and put them into my gym bag and then quietly went down
the backstairs, out the side door, and around to the street to
wait for the others. A few minutes later, Grams and Molly and
Dennie appeared. Dennie was carrying a suitcase.

"My wedding gown and your sisters' dresses," Grams explained.

"And my makeup and curling iron," Dennie added.

Bruce was waiting for us at the corner. He had borrowed his
father's car for the occasion. When he saw us, he backed up the
car so Grams wouldn't have to walk so far.

"Notice how quiet this car is?" he said happily. "Will Harold
have a problem leaving Cherry Garden so late?"

"Oh, he has it all planned." Grams settled herself in the back
seat. "He checked out for the night, so they won't be expecting

169

him back this evening. He went to dinner at his daughter's, but when they brought him back, he didn't sign in. He left a note in his room saying since he's of sound mind, he's leaving. He'll be waiting for us at the all-night Shop and Save market two blocks down from Cherry Garden."

When we pulled up in front of the market, Harold stepped out of the doorway. "Right on time," he said. He patted the back seat as he got in. "Nice car. Did you buy it for the occasion?"

Bruce grinned. "It's my dad's car, but my folks are away for Easter vacation."

"You didn't take it without their knowing, did you?" Grams asked.

"No, Dad left me the keys."

I bet he didn't think Bruce would drive it to Reno, though.

I slept most of the way. It's not a very interesting trip, and in the dark, it is less than nothing. We arrived around 6:00 a.m. I had never seen Reno before. It looked dingy, like something out of those old black-and-white movies. Some of the huge signs were on, but in the thin morning light, the colors looked washed out. The people on the streets had a rumpled, red-eyed look as if they had been up all night. It was too early to check into our hotel, so we went to a restaurant where we crammed ourselves into a booth and stared at one another.

"I can't believe we really did it," Grams said. "Do you think your father has missed us yet?"

"I imagine Mom will come looking for me to go running with her. Of course, it is vacation—maybe she was going to let me sleep in," Dennie said.

"I don't think they'll be worried," Molly added. "It's obvious we went somewhere together."

"I think we should phone home," Grams declared. "We're

safe now. Even if Christopher leaped into his car immediately, we'll be married by the time he finds us."

Grams opened her purse and took out her phone card. "Coming?" she said to Harold. "We might as well face the music."

After they left, the four of us ordered breakfast. While we were waiting, Molly asked, "Have you noticed there are some very strange people in this restaurant?"

I glanced over my shoulder and found myself staring into the eyes of what appeared to be a human-sized beetle with two aluminum-foil antennas. Sitting next to this thing was someone dressed in some kind of space uniform.

"Wow!" Bruce said. "What luck! There must be a science fiction convention in town."

Before I could comment, Grams and Harold came back and slipped into the booth.

"What happened?" Dennie asked.

"Not much," Grams said. "Although I didn't give your mother a chance to react. I announced that Harold and I were in Reno getting married and that you children were with us because you didn't want us to make such a long drive alone, and then I hung up."

"Just like that?" Molly asked. "I'd love to see Dad's face when Mom tells him."

Then Harold said, "Fortunately, I didn't have to talk to Sarah. Her husband answered the phone, so I told him where we were and that I'd get in touch with Sarah when I got back. He actually congratulated us. I hope he softens the blow when he tells her."

I felt a little let down. I had expected a few fireworks. I'd rather that everybody blew up right away and got it out of their systems before we got home.

After we ate, we went over to the hotel. It was still too early to sign in, so Harold went off to check our bags.

"Is that person wearing some new style?" Grams pointed to what appeared to be a large stuffed bear that had gotten stuck in a dryer walking across the lobby. "I've never seen so many bizarre outfits in my life. You would think it was Halloween."

"It's a science fiction convention," Bruce explained.

"What will they think of next?" Grams commented.

When Harold got back, he gave each of us five dollars. "I understand there are video rooms where you kids can play."

I heard Dennie sigh.

"You have to all stay together," Grams said.

Harold consulted his watch. "Let's say your grandmother and I will meet you in the lobby at eleven?"

I was about to start looking for the video room when Bruce grabbed the five dollars out of my hand. "You can play video games any old time. Let's see some of the convention. I saw a poster in the restaurant, and it's in the hotel across the street."

"Yeah," Molly said. "Dad wouldn't let me go to the science fiction convention they had in San Jose last year. I've always wanted to go to one."

"Why can't you guys go to the convention and I'll go to the arcade?" I said.

"Stop whining," Dennie told me. "Grams wants us to stay together."

I shrugged.

Even though it was early in the morning, everything was open and the streets were crowded. I could see into the gambling casinos with rows and rows of slot machines. At every machine stood a person. They looked like robots on an assembly line.

The convention wasn't open yet, but that didn't matter because we really didn't have enough money to buy tickets. There was a writer in the coffee shop who looked like he was trying to get people to ask him questions. Most people were too busy drinking their coffee to pay much attention to him. The displays all over the lobby advertised the different activities. Then Bruce noticed a hallway where some people were setting up tables and arranging artwork.

"Come on," Bruce said. "This is the artists' ghetto. That's where the artists go who can't afford to buy display space in the show."

We wandered down the corridor. I stopped at one of the tables where an artist was selling some sketches.

"Hey, Bruce," I said. "Gimme back my five dollars. I want to buy one of those drawings." I picked up the one I wanted. I was glad I'd brought some extra money.

"Let me see." Molly reached out and grabbed the drawing from my hand. "That's gross," she said. "It's not worth twenty dollars."

"Nobody asked you," I said.

At about a quarter to eleven, Dennie said, "Come on, we'd better go and meet Grams and Harold. She'll be worried if we're late."

As we crossed the street, we saw an ambulance, the red light on its roof pulsating, parked in the circular driveway of our hotel. Two orderlies were pulling a stretcher out of the back.

"Maybe there's a bomb threat," Molly said.

"Where do you get these ideas?" Dennie asked. "Besides, you don't need a stretcher for a bomb threat."

As we entered the lobby, we could see a crowd gathered around the main staircase. When we pushed our way through the people, we found Grams. She was bending over Harold, who was sprawled on the bottom stair. A girl dressed as a two-headed monster was saying, "I didn't shove him on purpose."

"Of course you didn't, dear," Grams said. "But you should be more careful. I'm sure you can't see properly with that thing on your head."

"Harold, are you all right?" Dennie knelt down beside him.

Harold nodded, but he looked pale and there were little beads of sweat on his upper lip.

"I think he's broken his ankle," Grams said.

"Again?" Molly said.

"What happened?" I asked.

"Nothing, really. We had gone up to our room to put the suitcase and your gym bag away, and we were coming back down the stairs to meet you children when this girl pushed past and Harold lost his balance and fell."

The medic and a policeman sat on the bottom stair next to Harold. "Are you having trouble breathing?" the medic asked. "Are you in any pain?"

Harold struggled to sit up. "Really, I'm fine. It's just my ankle."

The medic started to take Harold's blood pressure. "It's routine, sir," he said.

"Now, Harold," Grams said, "you just relax and do what the man wants."

"Grams, why don't you sit down?" Dennie tried to steer her toward a chair.

"I can sit in the ambulance," Grams said. She pulled at the arm of the policeman. "What hospital are you taking him to?"

"Good Samaritan," the policeman said.

"Could you tell my grandchildren how to get there, please. Bruce, listen to what the man says. Oh!" She suddenly noticed that Harold was being carried out. "I'll meet you at the hospital. And here's the key to our room if you need it for anything."

We watched Grams follow the stretcher out the door.

"I can't believe it," Molly said. "Do you think Harold has weak ankles or something?"

"Talk about being unlucky," Bruce said.

We trooped out of the hotel and went to the garage to get the car. Even with the directions the policeman had given us, Bruce got lost a couple of times before we arrived. We found Grams in the emergency room.

"Where's Harold?" I asked.

"They're setting his ankle," Grams said.

"It's not the same one, is it?" Molly plopped down beside her.

"No, it's the other one. Actually, I understand once a broken bone has healed, it's stronger than it was before. Of course," Grams added, "your mother would probably say that was an old wives' tale."

"Is he going to be okay?" I sat down next to Molly.

"The doctors didn't seem terribly concerned. His pulse is a little fast and his blood pressure is quite high, but they said that under the circumstances that wasn't surprising."

"Oh, Grams, we're sorry," Dennie said. "Everything seemed to be going so well."

"I'm beginning to think this was never meant to be," Grams said.

"Don't say that." Dennie patted Grams's hand.

It seemed as if we were there for hours before the door marked RESTRICTED: AUTHORIZED PERSONNEL ONLY opened and a doctor dressed in green pajamas came out.

"Are you Mrs. Wagner?" he asked.

"More or less," Grams said.

"We set the bone. It was an uncomplicated break. I'd like to keep him overnight, though, just to be on the safe side. They'll be taking him upstairs to his room in a few minutes. Any questions?" The doctor was already halfway out of the waiting room.

Grams got up and began gathering her coat and purse. "Coming?" she said to us.

"We'll be up in a minute," Dennie said.

"I guess you can ask at the information desk to find out what his room number is. Are you hungry?" Grams fished in her purse and pulled out a twenty-dollar bill. She gave it to Dennie. "Why don't you children pick up some sandwiches or something?"

"We've got to talk," Dennie said once Grams was out of hearing.

"Why?" I asked. "What's there to talk about? I think Grams is right. They were never meant to get married."

"I'm not giving up," Dennie said. "They have the license. We just have to ask Father Owens if he can come to the hospital for the ceremony."

"That's really romantic," Molly said. "Getting married in a hospital."

"Let's get something to eat," I suggested.

I was ignored.

"The first thing we have to do is phone Father Owens," Dennie said.

We went to the main lobby. Dennie found a bank of phones. "I need some change," she said.

I dug through my pockets and handed her a couple of dimes and two quarters. Then Molly and I sat down. After a few minutes, Dennie came back. "Father Owens will be right over.

Good thing the ambulance brought Harold to this hospital. Father Owens is a chaplain here."

"Can we get something to eat while we wait?" I asked.

"Forget your stomach," Dennie said. "We can't leave the lobby: we might miss him."

"Right over" to Father Owens seemed to mean an hour. I had read, cover to cover, six magazines before I looked up and saw a priest walking in the front door. Dennie got up and went to him. They stood talking for a few minutes. I admired the way Dennie was able to communicate with adults. I wondered if it was a skill that came with age or whether it was something you were born with. If you were born with it, I was out of luck.

Finally Dennie and Father Owens went to the information desk.

Molly and I followed them.

"His room is 621," the clerk was saying.

"Why don't you give me a few minutes alone with them?" Father Owens suggested to us.

We agreed. At my pleading, we went down to the basement, where the cafeteria was. Dennie didn't want to take the time to get a real meal, so we got some sandwiches out of a machine. It was better than nothing, but Dennie kept telling us to hurry up.

When we finished, we went up to Harold's room. We could hear Grams and Father Owens talking. I couldn't hear Harold, so I guessed he was still pretty much out of it. Finally Father Owens came out. He smiled at the four of us. "I think you can prepare for a wedding," he said. "I have to make several phone calls, change my schedule a little. And we need to give Harold more time to recover from the anesthetic. The nurses assured me that in a few hours he will be able to go to the chapel for the ceremony."

A minute later, Grams joined us. "You can come in and see him for just a minute," she said to us. "And then we're going to let him sleep for a while."

We tiptoed in. Harold was lying flat in the bed. There was a sort of cage over his ankle to keep the covers off his cast, and a bar trapeze arrangement hanging in front of him.

"I'm beginning to think Sarah is right," he said to us. "I'm totally incompetent. Maybe I do belong in Cherry Garden, where I can be watched."

"Nonsense." Grams started fussing with his pillow. "That's just the painkillers talking. Think of the story we'll have to tell our great-grandchildren. Now, you rest and take a nap. Father Owens is arranging to have the wedding here. The children and I are going over to the hotel to get dressed."

Harold's eyelids were already starting to close. Grams patted his cheek.

"He is all right?" I asked.

"Oh, yes," Grams said. "He's just slightly groggy from the medication. But the nurse said he'd be fully awake in a couple of hours. Come on. We have a wedding to get ready for."

ON THE WAY BACK TO THE HOTEL, BRUCE GOT
lost again.

"You just reverse directions," I said from the back seat.

"Shut up, kid," Bruce said.

Grams and the girls let me change into my slacks and good
sweater first. Bruce agreed to wait in the lobby, since he hadn't
brought other clothes. It only took me a few minutes. When
I started to leave, Grams came over. She pressed some money
and her camera into my hand.

"Will you buy some film in the gift shop?"

"Sure."

The gift shop was crowded. While I waited my turn, I
started looking around. Back against the wall was a re-
frigerated cabinet with fresh flower arrangements on display.

What's a wedding without flowers, I asked myself.

"Do you sell flower bouquets?" I said to the clerk.

"You mean an arrangement in a vase?" The clerk was busy searching on a shelf for my film.

"No," I said. "More like flowers a person could carry."

"You'll have to go to a florist for that," the clerk replied. "The shop that supplies us is down the street."

"How much would a small bouquet cost?" I asked.

The clerk shrugged. "Twenty dollars maybe, hard to tell."

I gulped and paid for the film. I realized I didn't have any money at all. I had spent it all on that drawing. I could ask Dennie and Molly or even Bruce to kick in some money, but I liked the idea of giving Grams her bridal bouquet myself. After all, I was giving her away. I should do something special. I went back up to the room and knocked on the door.

"Who is it?" Molly called.

"I have to come in for a minute."

"You can't," Molly said. "Grams isn't dressed yet. Dennie is doing her hair."

"Then pass out that bag with the drawing I bought. I left it on the table in the corner near the TV set."

"Why?" Molly asked. But in a minute she opened the door and handed me the bag.

I gave her the camera and film and took the bag and went across the street to the science fiction convention. I wasn't happy because I hate to return things. Even when clothes don't fit or there's something wrong with what I've bought, I'd rather keep it than make a fuss. If I'm desperate, I can usually get Ma to return my stuff.

I mentally ran through plausible reasons I might have for returning the sketch. I finally opted for being brutally honest because I couldn't think of anything else remotely believable.

"I need the money," I explained to the artist.

180

"Sorry, kid, do you see a sign anywhere that says 'Returns Accepted'?" the guy asked.

"I don't see a sign that says 'No Returns.' "

"Move on, kid, you're blocking my paying customers. A deal's a deal."

"Yeah, but I really do need the money back. It's for my grandmother and grandfather. Well, he will be my grandfather once he marries my grandmother. He's in the hospital."

"Twenty dollars won't buy you anything in a hospital. What kind of a scam are you trying to pull?"

"No scam, honest," I said. "But they're getting married in a couple of hours and I want her to have a bouquet of flowers. I'm giving her away."

"I thought you said he was in the hospital," the artist said.

"He is, but that's where they're getting married."

"Hey, give the kid his money back. Nobody could make up a story like that."

I suddenly realized that a crowd had gathered behind me and a total stranger was defending me.

"Yeah," somebody else said. "Don't be so cheap."

The crowd began making unfriendly noises. I hoped I hadn't started some kind of riot. I was relieved when the artist shrugged and opened the metal box on his table and pulled out a twenty-dollar bill and shoved it at me.

"Where's my sketch?"

"Here." I pushed the bag at him and grabbed the money. "Thanks!" I said to the stranger, who was dressed like Mr. Spock, complete with pointy ears.

"My pleasure, and may your grandmother live long and prosper," he said.

To my embarrassment, several others in the crowd offered

181

their congratulations, too. Somebody actually tried to press some money into my hand, but I shook my head. I wasn't taking up a collection.

The florist shop was right where the clerk had said. The man in the shop wasn't very helpful. "You want a bridal bouquet?" he asked. "That'll cost you about, oh, minimum fifty dollars, maybe a hundred."

I stared at him.

"There are samples in that book over there." He pointed to a glass table with a pile of books stacked on them.

"I don't want some huge thing," I said. "Something little." I remembered the flowers for Karen. "A little bigger than what girls wear on their wrist."

"I'll get my wife," the guy said. "She handles prom stuff."

His wife was more willing to listen. She didn't interrupt me when I explained what I wanted, and she didn't laugh when I told her how much I had to spend.

"You just wait here," she said. "I'm sure we have flowers left over from our Easter business." She disappeared behind a curtain.

While I waited, I paged through a book of bridal bouquets. I couldn't imagine Grams carrying around some of those monster arrangements. I began to hope that the woman understood that I wanted a small bouquet.

When she came back, she was carrying one that was bigger than Karen's but not the size of the examples in the book. There were different-colored flowers in it, and they were framed by paper that looked like lace. There was a handle sticking out the back.

"Now, isn't that pretty?" the woman asked me. "I hope your grandmother likes it." She started to put it into a box. "I made

182

a boutonniere for your soon-to-be-grandfather. He can pin it on his hospital gown." She added it to the box.

"Are you sure this is enough?" I handed her my twenty dollars.

She gave me the box. "Don't worry," she said.

"Thank you very much." I suspected she had thrown in a lot more than twenty dollars' worth of flowers. "Ah, could you put the box into a paper bag?" I hated to ask her for anything else, but I didn't want Dennie or Molly making fun of me, and besides, I wanted to surprise Grams.

When I got back to the hotel, everybody was waiting for me in the lobby.

"Where were you?" Molly asked.

Dennie spied the bag. "You went back to that silly convention and bought something else, didn't you?"

"Did you really think it was a silly convention?" Bruce asked Dennie.

Dennie ignored Bruce and kept staring at me. At least she had asked me a question I could answer honestly. I admitted that, yes, I had gone back to the convention. I didn't tell her why or where I went afterward.

"You should have found me," Bruce said. "I would have liked to see more."

"Let's go," Grams said.

On the drive back to the hospital, Bruce didn't get lost.

"Good job," I said.

Since we weren't going back to Harold's room, we stopped at the information desk to ask where the chapel was. When we got there, Harold was waiting for us in a wheelchair. Grams gave him a big kiss.

"You look much better," she said.

183

"I feel much better," he said. "Father Owens was just here. He's down at the nurses' station, but he said everything was arranged."

"So," Grams said, "this is it."

"Cold feet?" Harold asked.

"Not on your life. And at least I know you won't break your arm or anything walking down the aisle."

"Now, that was unnecessary," Harold said.

"Just kidding," Grams said. "Come on, Andy."

"Just a sec." I reached into the bag, pulled out the box, opened it, grabbed the boutonniere, and handed it to Harold. "I thought this would dress up that outfit."

"Why, Andy, thank you very much." Harold took the pin out of the back and fastened the flowers to the front of his hospital gown. "How do I look?" he asked.

"Very handsome," Dennie said.

When the nurse wheeled Harold toward the altar, I handed Grams the box with the bouquet in it.

She opened it and took out the arrangement. "Oh, Andy," she said. "I'm going to cry." She reached into the pocket of her coat for a handkerchief. "What a sweet, sweet thing to do." She leaned over and kissed me.

I backed away in embarrassment.

"Now." She took off her coat. She had on some lacy-looking dress that wasn't really white, but I don't know what color it was if not white.

"The flowers are perfect," Grams said and turned to greet Father Owens.

"All ready?" he asked. "Bruce, since you're the best man, you should be standing next to Harold. Do you have the rings?"

Bruce fished them out of his pocket and showed them to Father Owens.

"Good." Father Owens moved Molly and Dennie toward the door. "After you get in, Dennie, you should stand next to Bruce, since you two are the official witnesses. Molly, you come in ahead of Andy. Andy, you take your grandmother's arm and come in when I give you the nod."

My stomach began to feel strange. Maybe it was because I noticed that four or five nurses and a couple of people in bathrobes were gathering behind us. One nurse was aiming Grams's camera at us. Father Owens went into the chapel. He turned on a small tape recorder that was sitting on the altar. As the music started to play, Father motioned Molly and Dennie to start in.

Grams's hand started to tremble. I didn't know what else to do, so I squeezed it.

"It's okay, Grams," I said. "Harold's a really nice guy."

"I know," Grams whispered.

FOR ALL THE FUSS OF CHANGING CLOTHES AND GET-
ting film and flowers, it was a very short wedding. After I had
said "I do," when asked who gives this woman away, and
Grams and Harold said "I do" to Father Owens's questions, we
took Harold back to his room. The nurses tried to make it
special. One of them had gotten a small, flat cake that had BEST
WISHES written on it, and we all had a piece. Then the nurses
gave Harold a shot and started to get him ready for the night,
and we took Grams back to the hotel.

"I'll treat you to dinner," she said. "And then I want you
children to start back home. I'll be perfectly safe, and tomorrow Harold will be released, and when he feels up to it,
we'll fly home. Are you sure you'll be all right driving at
night?"

"We came up at night," Bruce pointed out.

"Yes, but you haven't had much sleep."

"Don't worry, Mrs. W.," Bruce said. "Staying up for eighteen hours is nothing. I always do it."

"I doubt that," Grams said. "Now, if you get tired, you pull over and let Dennie drive. Oh, dear, maybe you children should stay overnight. I don't know, I can't seem to think anymore."

"Grams, Grams," Dennie said. "Don't worry, we'll be fine. Anyway, I heard two of the bellboys talking, and there's the chance of a spring storm. So you see, we have to leave or we might get stuck up here."

"I have to get my father's car back," Bruce added.

"Then you'd better start now." Grams fumbled in her purse. "I'll give you money for dinner, and you can stop along the way."

"What about you?" Molly asked.

"I'll have something light delivered to my room," Grams said. "I'm not very hungry."

"Be sure to lock your door," Dennie said. "And don't open it unless you know who it is."

We left Grams standing in the lobby of the hotel waving and smiling at us.

I think we all felt let down. I know I did. It was like Christmas afternoon. You've opened all the gifts and you've gotten everything you really wanted, and yet it was over so quickly it was as if your mind couldn't catch up to the fact that it had come and gone.

When we left the hotel, we discovered the wind was starting to blow and black clouds were piling up on the horizon, so Bruce decided to wait and get dinner after we were out of the mountains. Dennie curled up in the front seat next to Bruce and went to sleep. Molly spread herself over more than her share of the back seat, wrapped herself in her jacket, and did the same.

Bruce and I drove in silence for a while. It was so quiet that I began to worry that Bruce might fall asleep.

"Do you think your parents will notice how many miles you've put on their car?" I leaned forward and rested my elbows on the back of the front seat. I figured talking might help keep him awake.

"I never thought of that," Bruce said. "Usually, with my car I don't pay any attention to that kind of stuff, but you're right. My father is a nut about maintenance, and he schedules oil changes and stuff on how many miles the car has gone."

He was quiet for a few minutes. "Well," he finally said, "I'll just tell him the truth. Otherwise, he'll suspect the worst."

I wondered what could be worse than driving his father's car up to Reno and back. "So," I said in an effort to keep the conversation going, "what are you going to do after you graduate?"

"I have a scholarship to U.C. Davis," he said.

"A scholarship?" I hadn't known Bruce was big in sports. In fact, I didn't remember him being on any team. "What in?"

"Chemistry," he said. "I plan to be a research chemist."

I was stunned.

"I was thinking of going into computers, I could have gotten a scholarship to Carnegie-Mellon for math—you make more money at that—but I figured I could do more good with research."

"Does Dennie know this?" I asked.

"Sure," he said. "Dennie supports me all the way. If she can wangle the financing, she'd like to go to Davis, too. Her specialty is marketing research."

I sat back to digest this piece of information. I knew last

November Dennie was sending out all these applications to college, but I hadn't paid much attention to whether she had been accepted anywhere. I figured she'd go to San Francisco State or maybe U.C. Berkeley and live at home.

"What are your plans?" Bruce asked.

"I haven't really thought about it much," I admitted.

Bruce grunted. "You'd be good at law," he said.

"I would? Why?"

"You like to argue," he said.

I considered that.

"Most of the time you seem to be pretty logical," Bruce continued. "You do have a tendency to try to get out of things, though. Maybe you should concentrate on business and specialize in middle management. My older brother was like you, always passing the buck, and when he went into business, he found he was good at delegating. The secret seems to be knowing when to stop. But he makes a good manager."

I wasn't sure I liked the turn the conversation had taken. And I was being forced to see Bruce in an entirely different light. I was glad when he decided he needed something to eat and drink to keep himself awake. After we had eaten, Dennie stayed awake, so that was the end of my conversation with Bruce.

It was after one in the morning when we got home. There were no lights on in the house. Bruce parked up the street, and Dennie, Molly, and I walked the block in silence. I noticed Bruce didn't drive away until he saw us unlock the side door and disappear into the garage.

Daisy heard us. We could hear her bark thundering through the house.

"So much for sneaking in," Dennie said.

"I didn't think we would be that lucky," I said.

When we got to the top of the stairs I discovered someone had locked my door from the inside. We could hear Daisy running back and forth. Molly and Dennie sat down on the top step. I rattled the doorknob. No point pretending we hadn't come home. Finally the door opened. Daisy flung herself at me. Then she raced down the stairs and back up again before she leaped on my bed.

"So," Pop said, "the prodigals return. I'm afraid I'm all out of fatted calves."

"Are you all right?" Ma asked.

We nodded.

Pop was looking over our shoulders. "Where is your grand-mother?"

"She's fine," Molly said. "Honest."

"I didn't ask how she was, I asked where she was," Pop answered.

"She and Harold stayed in Reno," Dennie said.

"Why didn't she come home with you?" Pop turned to Ma. "You told me that's what she said she was going to do when she phoned."

"Don't stand on the stairs," Ma said. "Come in."

We filed through my room and went into the kitchen.

"Why is she still in Reno? How will she get home?" Pop demanded.

"Harold is in the hospital, but only for overnight," I explained.

"He'll be out"—Molly looked at her watch—"today, I guess. So they decided to stay a few days and then fly home. They'll let you know."

"That's awfully decent of them," Pop said.

"What's the matter with Harold?" Ma asked.

"He broke his other ankle," I said. "But it wasn't Grams's fault. Actually, it wasn't his fault, either. Someone bumped into him on the stairs."

"Is this what my mother can look forward to, one broken bone after another?" Pop asked. "Next it will be his arms, I suppose. Better he should break his neck!"

"Now, that is enough," Ma said.

"When did he break his ankle?" Pop asked.

"When?" Dennie repeated.

"Yes, when. When you first got there, or after"—he paused—"they were married."

"Oh, it was before," Molly said. "They had gotten their license and they were waiting for us at the hotel and that's when he fell."

"So they didn't get married?" Pop sounded hopeful.

I waited a minute, but when nobody spoke, I said, "They were married at the hospital."

"Oh, you should have seen it," Molly said. "It was so romantic. The priest was willing to do it there."

"Well, wasn't that convenient," Pop commented. "And where did this priest come from?"

"I'm tired. Can't we talk about this in the morning?" Dennie said.

"Of course we can," Ma said.

Before Pop could say anything else, Dennie and Molly ran out of the kitchen. I made a move toward my room.

"Why did you do it?" Pop asked me. "I made no secret of how I felt."

I expected that question, and I had thought about how I'd answer it. I knew why I'd done it, but I wasn't sure I could explain it. Maybe I could pretend ignorance: "Do what?" or innocence: "What'd I do?" or defiance: "I didn't do anything."

191

I took a deep breath. I wanted to be sure I got it right, or I'd be in even bigger trouble.

"It seemed to me that Grams and Harold had a right to do what they wanted. In this class at school we've been discussing basic human rights and civil disobedience. If people's rights are taken away, it's okay if they break the law to get them back, because there's something like a higher law. I think that's what it's called. Actually, Grams and Harold didn't break the law, I was thinking of what the rest of us did, although that wasn't really breaking the law either." I took a deep breath. I felt as if I was going down for the third time. "I can't explain it."

"Bishop Alemany is encouraging you students to break the law?"

"No, not exactly." I might have known he'd zero in on one small detail and ignore the main point. I tried to remember Mr. Clark's lecture. "I mean, not any old law."

"Do you hear that?" Pop waved his hand. "Do you hear what he said?"

Ma didn't answer.

"First that school encourages our daughter to marry a cretin like Bruce and now they're telling our son to become a criminal."

"That's not quite accurate," I interrupted. "What you said about Bruce. He's smarter than we thought."

"Why, Andy," Dennie said. I hadn't realized she had returned to the kitchen. She was standing next to Ma. "I'm surprised to hear you say that. I didn't think you liked Bruce."

"I thought you were tired and went to bed," Pop said.

"I didn't think it was fair for Andy to take all the flak," Dennie said.

"Bruce's a pretty sharp guy," I said. "I got to know him better on the trip."

"We are not talking about Bruce," Pop shouted.

"You were the one who mentioned him," Dennie pointed out.

"Chris, stop for a minute," Ma said. "Listen to me. Do you remember when you asked me to marry you?"

"Now you're changing the subject," Pop accused her.

"As I recall," Ma continued, "my mother and father wanted us to wait for a while. I think the word they used to describe you was 'impetuous.' 'Improvident' was also tossed around. I'm afraid my father hoped we'd wait forever. Anyway, what did you say to me when I told you what they thought?"

"Liz, that was almost twenty years ago."

"I remember," Ma said. "You said that we were both adults and we had a right to make our own choices."

"That was different," Pop said. "Your father took some kind of irrational dislike to me." Pop looked around at the three of us. "Why is it impossible for this family to stay focused on one thing? You people have minds like gnats." He walked off.

We looked at Ma. "I think your father has just heard himself talking. Give him time to digest it. It was probably a blessing in disguise that Harold broke his ankle. This way, your father will have time to cool off before they get home," Ma said.

I agreed. As he left, Pop had looked more confused than angry.

"If that's the end of the discussion, I'm going to bed," Dennie said. "And I'll watch the twins tomorrow."

"Did Pop really say that about the right to make choices?" I asked Ma. "Why didn't you say that before? It sounds like a pretty good argument to me."

Ma shrugged. "I had hoped he would think of something like that himself. Actually, Grandpa and Grandma didn't really have anything against your father; they thought I was too young. But that isn't important. What is important is that your father rethink his position."

"I still don't understand why he's making such a federal case out of Grams getting married again."

"Oh, I think I know," Ma said. "Grams and Grandfather were very busy when your father was a little boy. They were always traveling. This is the first real family life he's ever known. Sometimes he has trouble understanding that families are expandable. Give him time. He'll see that Grams loves him just as much even though she has Harold. I'm sure he'll finally accept Harold. Eventually he might even get to like Bruce."

I laughed. "That'll be the day."

"So much has changed this year," Ma said. "It's hard to believe. Dennie will be off to college in less than a year, and the twins are in school. No wonder your father went off the deep end. I never met anyone who resists change the way he does."

"Tell me about it."

"You must be exhausted." Ma leaned up and gave me a quick kiss on the cheek. "Good night."

When Ma left, I went to my room and began to wonder if maybe I was like Pop. "Hey," I said to Daisy, who was nosing around my feet. "Do you think it's time I changed my image?"

Daisy didn't respond. She leaped onto the bed and thumped her tail. I got undressed, pulled on my gym shorts, and lay down on the bed. Families were strange things, I thought. The best part was that you didn't get thrown out no matter how stupidly you behaved. The worst part was people felt very free to criticize you. In the long run I supposed it all evened out.

Daisy nuzzled my neck before she sighed and stretched out next to me. The nice part about dogs, I concluded, is that they don't expect anything of you, but then they are awfully dependent. I'd hate to wait around until someone remembered to feed me.

The next morning I met Dennie in the hallway. She was coming out of the bathroom and I was going in.

"Dad wasn't as mad as I thought he would be," Dennie said.

"Let's just hope this is the end of it," I said.

"I meant to tell you, I was impressed. Giving Grams those flowers," she said. "I might even use the word 'sensitive.'"

"Hey, haven't you heard," I replied, "I'm a caring kind of guy?" Maybe I was stretching the truth a little, but I was in there trying. Who knows what I'd be like in a few years.

PROPERTY OF
FRANKFORT HIGH SCHOOL